
★

On the floor, between the settee and the fireplace, lay the remains of Julia Henderson. One leg was bent beneath her. Trying not to gulp for air, Ian Roper gripped the back of an armchair and tried to pull himself together. He did not want to show himself up in front of his subordinates. He was used to the sight of death, but it never ceased to nauseate him. Besides, it was not usually as ugly as this. The fact that the woman had been murdered was not open to doubt. Suicides did not beat their brains out.

★

"Murderous passions simmer...in this fine mystery debut."

—*Publishers Weekly*

D0366856

JANIE BOLITHO

Kindness can kill

WORLDWIDE ®

TORONTO • NEW YORK • LONDON
AMSTERDAM • PARIS • SYDNEY • HAMBURG
STOCKHOLM • ATHENS • TOKYO • MILAN
MADRID • WARSAW • BUDAPEST • AUCKLAND

For Jim, without whom this would
not have been possible

KINDNESS CAN KILL

A Worldwide Mystery/February 1996

First published by St. Martin's Press, Incorporated.

ISBN 0-373-26193-4

Printed in U.S.A.

Acknowledgment

To PC Paul Clark of Slough Police for his
patience and humor

ONE

THE REVEREND Michael Barfoot looked down on his congregation and sighed. His mind was not where it should be, here in his church. He chided himself. How could he expect others to believe, how could he possibly expect to increase attendances if he himself could not concentrate? He wished yesterday had never existed. St Luke's was never full, those days were long gone, but his parish was large and enough pews were filled to require the services of a full-time vicar rather than one whose time was divided between several smaller churches.

Today he noted the extra gaps. The weather he supposed. Spring and autumn were the best seasons for a record turn-out. Spring because the nearby beaches did not yet beckon and autumn when the inefficient heating still proved adequate. Although it was still April he calculated the temperature might reach the seventies by afternoon. The muggy drizzle of yesterday had given way to a clear, blue sky and he didn't blame people for choosing the beach in preference to a church service. Of course, yesterday's wedding also accounted for some of the absentees. And yesterday was when it all started. He looked around for his wife, as if to reassure himself she really existed.

The previous day, at four o'clock, Michael officiated at the largest marriage ceremony his church had witnessed for more than a decade. It was a match between two local, wealthy families, the Morleys and the Sutcliffs. When he learned of the engagement of Helen and Johnny he expected Caroline Morley to pick a grander setting for the occasion, for he knew Caroline well enough to realize her daughter would have no say in the matter. St Luke's was pretty enough in its lichen-covered way and artful photography would show the bride and groom posed in the lych-gate without revealing the flapping washing pegged to the rows of rotary lines belonging to the blocks of council flats beyond the cemetery.

Despite some initial nervousness on Michael's part, the ceremony passed without a hitch. The church was gratifyingly bursting at the seams and the flowers were magnificent. The reception, for as long as he stayed, seemed equally successful and he'd been surprised to discover quite a mixture of guests, not just other wealthy families. Naturally he knew most of the local people and had made the acquaintance of a few more. Ian Roper was one such person. Michael liked him and wished the man had not left so early as he was enjoying their conversation. He could not know that he was to meet him again in quite different circumstances.

Susan Barfoot, his wife, stayed until the end. Later, she told him, things had livened up and there was dancing. By eleven the whole thing was considerably noisier. Hangovers, therefore, accounted for some of his missing flock.

But this morning it was not the empty seats but Susan who disturbed his concentration. Dennis Morley stood up to read the Lesson. Michael tried to direct his mind to the words he not only heard but believed in. It was difficult. He could not stop thinking about what might have happened after he left the party. And what might have happened had he stayed.

He was in the process of completing a post-grad course at Saxborough when he met Susan. She was in her first year then, reading History. For reasons he would never comprehend she gave up the course to marry him. He never regretted it, he loved her and, he was certain, she had saved him from the problems of conscience he was suffering, and still suffered occasionally. He did not believe she regretted it either, until lately. Although she was as conscientious as ever in her duties as a vicar's wife, he sensed a restlessness in her. This morning, for instance, the one day she normally gave it a miss, she insisted on hoovering and dusting before she came to church. In comparison with other wives Susan always came out best and every day he thanked God for sending her to him. Not only did she look after him and the boys and the house with apparently effortless ease and efficiency, she was also beautiful. Straight blonde hair fell to her shoulders and her skin was almost translucent. She gave the impression of being delicate, so slim and small-boned that when he held her she reminded him of a small bird. If her passion had not matched his own he would have been terrified of crushing her when they made love. But she would have none of his protectiveness and the strength of her personality astounded him at times. To Michael it was no surprise that her best friend was Julia Henderson. Julia was her equal. As beautiful, but in a blatantly sexually-attractive way, the perfect foil for Susan's more ethereal looks, and she was as strong. Julia had needed to be to cope with the disappointments and tragedy in her life.

Michael returned to the pulpit and the service continued. Now his mind was on higher things as he gave
his sermon wholeheartedly. Once he became aware of
rustling and fidgeting. Tom Prendergast started it with
his coughing. He was a cunning old boy, and it was his
way of saying he was not too keen on the sermon.
Perhaps next week he would make it up to him, treat
him to some of the Old Testament fire and brimstone
of which he was so enamoured. In fact, it might do
them all some good. It might even do himself some.
He reached the section of his sermon written especially with Julia Henderson in mind. Many of the
townspeople treated her like a pariah, she would appreciate the reference.

From the Prayer Book he quoted 'Good Lord, de-
liver us from all blindness of heart, from pride, vain-
glory and hypocrisy'; stressing the last word pointedly. A few sentences later he threw in a line or two
from Paradise Lost, 'For neither man nor angel can
discern hypocrisy, the only evil that walks invisible,
except to God alone', and decided that although he
might have overdone it, the message was clear enough.
As the organist played the opening bars of a hymn, he
looked around to give Julia a quick wink and saw she
wasn't there. Another casualty of the wedding reception no doubt. It was a shame. He liked her as much
as Susan did and they both worked hard to try to bring
her name into conversations, showing their approval
so others could follow their example. They also involved her in things he suspected she wanted no part
of but was too kind to refuse. Somehow they never
managed to break down the barriers which prevented
other women befriending her. Their jealousies and

their prejudices were too strong. Julia was undeniably beautiful. Men lusted after her and their wives knew they did. Her looks alone were enough to arouse envy but coupled with the fact that she lived alone, the recipe for adultery was perfect. Few wives were prepared to take the risk of inviting her into their homes. Susan had done so, but Michael was trained in the art of fighting temptation.

Last Sunday, for example, Julia had wafted into church in a haze of mink and expensive perfume. There was much tut-tutting and head shaking on the part of the females but their partners were enjoying surreptitious glances at her legs and the hint of cleavage visible in the folds of fur. Only the Barfoots knew the coat was purchased in an Oxfam shop and she dressed that way deliberately.

'They expect it. And secretly they love it' she confided whilst sipping a coffee in Susan's kitchen before the service. 'Why disappoint them?' And she'd laughed her throaty, seductive laugh.

It was useless. Michael gave in and let his mind wander. He'd got through the hardest part, the sermon, without drying up but even the ritualistic words he spoke now couldn't soothe him. His eyes went to the back of the church.

Despite the brightness of the morning, Gerry Clayton sat in shadow. His expression was not discernible but the way in which he sat suggested he was alert, apparently taking in all he heard. Michael guessed correctly that the woman beside him was his wife.

It was only twenty-four hours since he was introduced to the man and he'd already seen him twice since. And why the sudden appearance in church if it wasn't for Susan?

Yesterday lunchtime Michael had left the Wheatsheaf where he called in for a quick pint before meeting Susan outside the supermarket to help her carry the shopping back to the vicarage. It was a five-minute walk, not worth the trouble of getting the car out and having to pay to park it. For some unknown reason the traffic wardens seemed more vigilant on Saturdays and even pausing briefly on the double yellow lines outside Fine Fare was enough to bring one striding down the street. Between the posters displaying special offers on the plate-glass window, he spotted the back of Susan's head. She stood with a full trolley, chatting to someone. Michael went in to give her a hand. She looked surprised to see him as if she did not realize how late it was, then, stammering slightly in confusion, introduced the man with whom she had been in deep conversation. His name was Gerry Clayton.

Susan explained that Gerry and his wife were new arrivals to Rickenham Green and that they had moved into a house on the estate where Julia lived. 'And,' she continued, turning back to the tall, craggy man at her side, 'in case you haven't heard already through the grapevine, Michael is the vicar of St Luke's.'

'Yes. Hello there.' Gerry extended his hand, the non-committal answer conveying nothing. Was there a slight tightening around his jaw as he spoke? Michael wasn't sure but he felt his interruption was unwelcome.

'Big do on this afternoon then.' Gerry seemed to be trying to make up for his initial surliness.

'You know about it?'

'Yes. I work for Dennis Morley. Ann and I have been invited, but only to the reception. I hear the church isn't big enough for all the people they wanted to invite.'

'No. Ah, well, good' was the best Michael could come up with, then he made all the usual platitudes of welcome and reminded Susan it was getting late and they ought to pay for the groceries and go and get ready. That was the extent of their first meeting. Nothing was said or done to indicate Susan and Gerry had been enjoying anything other than a casual chat, the sort she had all the time with various of his parishioners. But the blush gave her away, and the hesitation as she made the introductions worried Michael and then, afterwards, she had been strangely quiet. That alone was enough to arouse his suspicions. He could not help but be aware that other men found his wife attractive, but Susan was loyal and sensible, she wouldn't do anything to harm him and the boys. As far as he was aware she had never shown any signs of reciprocation to the passes she must surely receive.

But he could not get Gerry Clayton off his mind. All night he was tortured by the thought that this time she might have been tempted. The man was good looking in a rugged sort of way. And she had insisted on staying on at the reception when he wanted nothing more than a quiet night at home. They couldn't both stay, they had no babysitter. Now Matthew was fifteen they left him to look after Josh occasionally, but never later than eight or nine o'clock. And where was Matthew this morning? No. That was another issue, something to be dealt with later. Last night he had been more than fair. Susan did not get out very often and spent most of her time helping him with his work; he could not deny her the chance of a bit of fun. So, he decided, if his unreasonable feelings were going to interfere with his vocation there was no alternative but to confront Susan. Tonight, he determined, he would say something, if only to hear her laugh and tell him not to be so stupid. He was ashamed of himself for not conquering the un-Christian emotion of jealousy but he could also see why Julia had such a hard time of it if this is what the wives felt.

The congregation rose to sing the closing hymn. Susan was four rows from the front, her hair held back neatly in a pony tail tied with ribbon. Mote-filled sunshine danced off the gleaming strands of her hair and as the organ swelled she turned her head to glance behind her. Michael's stomach churned. He loved her so very much, he could not bear the thought of losing her.

As if sensing his thoughts, she looked up and smiled. Temporarily his fear subsided and his voice gained strength as he sang. He returned the smile, knowing everything was going to be all right.

BRADLEY COURT, the housing estate at one end of the High Street, was quiet. It was a typical Sunday afternoon. Most of the residents on the estate were commuters and travelled to Ipswich to work, but today, instead of enjoying the relative peace of their own gardens, many had gone off for the day and not yet returned. The only sounds to disturb the afternoon were those of birdsong and the buzz of a lawnmower further down Ash Farm Road. It was not near enough to cause annoyance to Gerry and Ann Clayton as they sat on their newly built patio soaking up the warmth of an early spring. They exchanged the usual comments about the unseasonal weather, how last summer they were not able to sit outside so late in the day without a cardigan, and made other desultory small talk. Then they went back to their individual thoughts.

On the wrought-iron table between them lay a couple of books and several sections of the *Sunday Times*. After church, which for once Gerry had attended with Ann, although she didn't go every week, they had had a pub lunch, which they ate in the garden of the Three Feathers at the opposite end of the High Street. Gerry was disappointed not to see Julia. She was there last week, and the week before that, when he and Ann first met her. She was a looker all right. And her smile. It had hit him straight in the groin. He knew he would never do anything about it. Once he might have, but not now.

Ann glanced at her watch then stood up saying she was going to make a sandwich.

'You don't want anything cooked I take it?' she inquired as she folded the newspaper back into its original shape.

'God, no thanks. Not after that lunch. I wouldn't mind a glass of that plonk though, if there's any left.'

'There's still three bottles. Are you sure?' Ann smiled. The case of wine was a leaving-cum-house-warming present from the school where she taught before they moved to Rickenham Green. It was the stuff they drank in the staff room on birthdays and at the end of term when the last of the kids had left the building, and it was pretty awful. Yet she and Gerry were getting through it at quite a rate, apart from what they bought from the off licence.

'I know, why don't I nip across and see if Julia wants to give us a hand to drink it?'

A furrow appeared in Ann's forehead, but before she disappeared into the house she replied in a level voice, 'Yes, why don't you.' She hoped Julia was out.

Gerry walked the few yards to the end of Ash Farm Road and turned into Churchill Way where Julia lived, whistling in anticipation as he did so. He could do with some cheerful company and Julia was certainly that. Ann was a bit down at the moment. He didn't blame her. How could he? He was the sole cause of her unhappiness.

He knocked on the door of number two and for the second time that Sunday was disappointed to discover he would not be enjoying Julia's company after all. There was no reply. He knocked again for good measure in case, like themselves, she was in the back garden, then gave up and walked home. She was definitely out. She could not have failed to hear his second knock, it reverberated through the still, warm air all the way back to where Ann stood in the kitchen buttering some bread.

At the time Gerry noticed nothing unusual, but he wasn't expecting to. He decided to make an effort with Ann. If he took the initiative for a change he could try to cheer her up. He knew he relied on her too much to provide his happiness.

Between them Gerry and Ann finished a bottle of wine with their snack, then started on a second. He had not been terribly successful in improving her mood and sensed his bluff attempts at heartiness was not the way to do it. They finished the second bottle of wine. Each had their own reasons for wishing to blot out the recent past. Not least of which was the cause of their move from London to Rickenham Green.

MICHAEL MADE USE of every minute of Sunday afternoon, willing the time to pass quickly. The four of them had eaten Susan's delicious lunch, then the boys went off to play. Or rather Josh, who was ten, did. Michael was not sure what Matthew did. For all the communication he received these days was by way of grunts and monosyllabic responses. He was well aware the boy was at an awkward age and that he would grow out of it; meanwhile he had to be content that he neither smoked, drank, nor took drugs and was not in any kind of trouble. As far as he knew his son's leisure hours were spent in the company of similar young men who also took pleasure in hanging around McDonalds or sitting in the bus shelter for hours on end discussing heaven knew what. His mother wasn't worried, and that was the main thing. She kept a firm and strict check on the boys and her reaction to them was an accurate gauge by which to measure their behaviour.

After repairing a puncture on Josh's bicycle, Michael cut back the untidy mess of a late-flowering clematis which trailed up the fence at the side of the vicarage and divided it from the road. Long, green shoots were tangled amongst last year's woody growth. As he carefully untwined fragile tendrils and pushed them to one side before wielding the secateurs, he rehearsed what he would say to Susan. Despite his efforts to keep himself occupied it still seemed an age before he was able to wave good-bye to the last of the Evensong congregation as they went off to their homes. And at last Josh was safely in bed and Matthew in his room listening to his cassette player. Only then was he free to join his wife in the sitting-room.

Unlike the accommodation at his last living, where draughts invaded every corner, this room was warm and cosy, centrally heated when necessary, and lit by soft lamps. Tonight, though, it was warmer than usual because the sun had streamed in through the French windows. It was a relief; the heating was an extravagance and they had always had to watch every penny.

Michael carried an open bottle of Medoc, their Sunday night treat and Susan's favourite wine, and two glasses and set them down on the sideboard.

'Drink?' he asked quietly, steadily, as if this was any Sunday evening.

'Yes, love one.' Susan replied without looking up from the magazine she was reading. Michael poured the drinks and wondered how to begin. So much for the rehearsals earlier in the afternoon.

'By the way, the new people, the Claytons, I saw them in church this morning. At least, I assumed the lady with him was his wife.' He hoped he sounded casually conversational. 'How long did you say they've been here?'

Susan's expression revealed nothing. She put down the magazine and taking the glass he offered, reached for a packet of cigarettes which lay on the table beside her.

'Oh, I don't think I did say. About a month.' She tilted her head back and blew out a trail of smoke which hid her face from her husband's anxious eyes. 'Well, Gerry has anyway, Ann's only been here a couple of weeks, she had to work out a month's notice.'

'What does he do? For a living I mean? Didn't he mention something about the Morleys? I meant to ask him last night but I didn't get a chance to speak to him.' This was not strictly true. For some reason Michael decided not to make the opportunity. Instead he watched to see how the man reacted to Susan's presence. He had been disappointed, if that was the word to use, to notice that if they did not actually avoid each other, they made very little contact. However, he had no idea of what might have occurred after he left and Susan had been very late home. But the man's wife was with him, or at least, the same woman who accompanied him to church, so his suspicions were probably unfounded. He thought his questions were beginning to sound more like an interrogation than a conversation. But Susan was not being very forthcoming, and his own guilt was mixed up with everything else. Not that he had done anything, or ever would. It was just that sometimes in the presence of attractive women, especially Julia, he found himself mentally undressing them, wondering what it would be like to have sex with them and his self-disgust was enormous. He was a man of the cloth. True, he was not expected to be celibate, but with a wife like Susan surely no man should be having such thoughts.

'Yes. He does work for the Morleys,' Susan said, 'well, for Dennis. Some sort of manager's job. You know Dennis, likes everything run for him, always the gentleman farmer, won't get his hands dirty for anyone.'

It was frustrating. Michael was learning nothing he did not already know.

'Susan?' After seventeen years of marriage, Susan knew his every tone of voice, certainly well enough to recognize the thinly disguised note of pleading in the question. She also guessed from his inquiries exactly what was troubling him. She was aware, too, how little he knew her.

'Michael, are you . . . ?' She paused, her grey eyes steady. 'This is about my talking to Gerry in Fine Fare, isn't it?'

As always, where he failed, Susan managed to come straight to the point. By bringing his fears into the open she consequently dissolved them.

She stood up, smiling tightly, and shook her head. 'Oh, Michael, I don't believe it. You're jealous. And after all these years.' Her lips were balm as she kissed him, first on the cheek then on the mouth, softly but persuasively, until he had no choice but to put down his glass of wine and kiss her back. He was wrong, so very wrong. How could he possibly have suspected her? He automatically thanked the God he loved and the tension drained away. He felt her fingers on his chest as she unbuttoned the shirt he'd changed into after the service and was excited in a way he would not have thought possible earlier. Within seconds they were both partially undressed and lying on the settee, making love with a passion that had been missing, at least on Susan's side, for several weeks. The boys, upstairs, were for the moment forgotten.

Later, he stroked her hair and laughed at their undignified disarray. Thankfully Matthew had not been able to tear himself away from his music and Josh had not come down on the pretext of wanting a glass of water.

Michael did not see how expertly she had diverted him from asking a direct question and thereby avoiding having to give him an answer.

TWO

PC Stone and PC Jackson were patrolling the early evening streets of Rickenham in their car when the call came over the radio. Nothing much was going on and although it sounded like a waste of time, they went off to investigate. It would relieve the boredom of this part of their shift. Later, once the pubs started turning out, there would be the usual assortment of drunk-and-disorderlies, or even a fight. Later still, when the tatty premises that had the audacity to call itself a nightclub closed, anything could happen.

Peter Jackson reversed into the opening where the lorries pulled in to unload their goods for Boots the Chemist and drove in the opposite direction to which they were heading.

Fifteen minutes later they knew this was no ordinary shift, that they'd be lucky to get off duty on time.

PC Stone left the house he had entered, careful not to touch anything and further confuse the fingerprint men, and spoke to headquarters over the car radio.

'The Chief's not going to like this,' Detective Sergeant Barry Swan said to himself as he picked up the telephone to contact him. Barry would not normally have been in his office so late but his recent promotion had given him an incentive to clear up some of the paperwork which was hanging around. His Chief had, as he always did, left a number where he could be contacted but also the instructions that it was only to be used in a dire emergency. This, Barry considered, counted as such.

'OH, GREAT FOOTBALL,' Ian Roper said, 'terrific left foot he's got. I told you it'd be a good game.' Ian's son, Mark, looked down at his damp trainers and sighed. It was not only his trainers which were damp and he was bored and uncomfortable and all because at fourteen he was flexing his muscles and refused to bring a coat with him. The false spring of the past few days had reverted to rain and chilly nights. For weeks now Dad kept promising to spend some time with him, to take him out somewhere, just the two of them. When he was younger he enjoyed the fact that his father was a detective, it was glamorous and impressed his schoolfriends, but now he wondered if the job was more important than himself.

Fair enough, for once Dad kept his promise and arrived home at five thirty to take him out, but Mark was not that keen on football and it irked him that his father supported Norwich City when Ipswich was not only nearer but also in their own county. He was pedantic about such things, just as Ian was about his work, and because of this, arguments ensued, neither realizing they arose because they were similar and this was one of the traits they had in common. The match they were watching was the last mid-week draw before cup final day so it was unlikely Mark could get the chance to watch Ipswich, with whom, he reasoned, his loyalties would lie, if he liked football, that is. And because his more sports-minded friends were Ipswich supporters they wouldn't be interested in where he'd been. The stirrings of adolescent rebellion were making themselves felt. Mark sullenly ignored his father's comments and asked if he could have a burger.

It was while he was queuing that he heard the announcement over the tannoy system and he felt tears prick behind his eyelids. So he was not to have even one night out. It was so bloody unfair, why couldn't they leave him alone. For a few seconds Mark wondered if he had the nerve to 'disappear', to make it difficult for his father to find him. He knew he wouldn't leave the ground without him. But the moment passed. He was brought up with the constant knowledge that Ian could be called away at any time, that it might be a matter of life or death and his disobedience could endanger someone's life. Mark dutifully left the short queue and returned to where Ian was waiting, his car keys already in his hand.

'Sorry, son. Tonight of all nights.' Mark saw his father was as pissed off as he was but for different reasons; he'd genuinely been enjoying the game. At the telephone box near the turnstiles Ian dialled the number for Rickenham police station. The conversation was brief. He replaced the receiver and stepped outside.

'We're going to have to step on it. I'm sorry about this. I'll make it up to you soon.' Together they walked quickly back to where the car was parked, Mark's only consolation was he had, for half an hour, seen that a detective could be just as much a boy as himself as his father had shouted and groaned along with the rest of the crowd. It proved he was human.

Whereas only last week Moira Roper had accused her husband of being just the opposite. 'How long is it since you've spent even an hour of your time with the boy?' she asked. 'He misses you, you know. It's inhuman the way you treat him, making promises then breaking them.'

'It's the job, love.' Ian used the words that over the years developed into a stock response, the words too easily summoned up to avoid a confrontation.

'Oh, of course, the job. It's always the bloody job. He needs you, Ian. Can't you see that?' Moira turned away; there were tears in her eyes and Ian knew this was serious. He could not recall the last occasion he heard his wife swear.

Ian pulled out of the side road in which he was parked and headed back towards Rickenham, driving fast but carefully. Had his son not been in the car he suspected he would have driven even faster. He sensed the boy's mood and tried to talk him out of it but Mark was not having it. He remained silent for the rest of the journey.

Carrow Road was several miles behind them. Ian's mind was not yet on the job ahead as he had only heard the barest details and it was no use speculating until there were hard facts in front of him. He wondered what Moira would say when he dropped Mark off at home. Well, she couldn't accuse him of not making an effort, it was just dreadful timing. Moira would understand that. He knew how hard it was for her, the untasted meals, cancelled nights out, the parties she occasionally attended unescorted, but he had made it very clear before they were married what their life together would be like, and he was ambitious and nothing, except his annual holidays, could be guaranteed. Moira was by no means unintelligent. She made her choice accepting the conditions, knowing part of the reasons she loved the man were because he was hard-working and dedicated and fully believed in what he was doing. She supposed, in those early days that, given an ultimatum, Ian would have chosen his career over her. Now, she was less certain. But sometimes he forgot he was a father as well as a husband. Even so it was a good marriage, despite irregular hours and telephone calls at any hour of the day or night. Surprisingly, these occurred more, rather than less often, with each promotion and were more than once the cause of some irritability over the breakfast table.

Ian took a bend too fast and made a conscious effort to slow down. A few extra minutes would make no difference now. His knuckles were white as he gripped the wheel hard and he knew he must relax; that he was putting his own, his son's and other motorists' lives in danger.

He breathed in deeply through his nose and out through his mouth several times, then tensed and untensed his shoulders. That was better. He knew he should do it more often. A couple of months ago he attended a psychology lecture, unwillingly, but feeling it was his duty to go, as the staff under him had been requested to do so. The request was a lightly veiled order.

First impressions showed Brian Lord, the psychologist, to be the stereotype imagined by Ian. He was bearded, his brown hair in need of a trim and sporting corduroy slacks and a polo-necked jumper. Ian sat back, arms folded, waiting to be proved right, for Mr Lord, he was sure, was about to embark on a sob story about poor, misunderstood criminals who, not having a childhood where every wish they expressed was gratified, turned to a life the wrong side of the law. Ian's jaw had tightened as, belligerently, he thought it was his mission to catch them, not rear them from babyhood.

Within a few minutes his scepticism vanished and he found himself leaning forward listening attentively.

During the hour throughout which he spoke, Brian Lord made no mention of crime or criminals, other than the effect they produced on the men and women who constantly came into contact with them. Instead he talked of the stress involved in police work, how witnessing violence on a daily basis could brutalize people, that long hours and lack of sleep caused tension in the home, sometimes enough to break up a marriage, and how this same stress—and here Ian listened even more attentively—was sometimes the cause of impotence.

Mr Lord went on to suggest that no matter how busy or involved in a case they became, they should always make time for their partner and children. More importantly, they should try to make time for themselves.

The lecture finished with a short demonstration of simple relaxation techniques, which Ian promised himself he would practise regularly. Until this evening he had forgotten. He was not, it appeared, very good at keeping his word.

He indicated left and shot across the roundabout at the end of the dual carriageway which led into the town centre. The High Street was quiet and within minutes he pulled up outside 14 Belmont Terrace. Mark jumped out and walked the few paces to the front door, put his own doorkey in the Yale lock and went inside without turning round. Now was not the time for worrying about his son. Ian shot back down the road and headed straight for headquarters. He parked in his allocated space in the carpark and started towards the main doors. There was already a car and driver waiting for him.

'Thought it would save a bit of time, sir,' Detective Sergeant Baker said. 'I can give you the details on the way.' Ian jumped into the passenger seat. 'Everyone relevant been notified?' he asked.

'Yes, sir, all taken care of.' Baker replied calmly. A veteran of thirty years, compared with his senior officer's twenty-three years in the force, he was a man who thought there was nothing new in the world.

He was wrong. Not even the staunch William Baker was prepared for the sight which awaited them.

They pulled in between a patrol car and an unmarked Jaguar and made their way to the open door of number 2, Churchill Way. Already there were people standing in their doorways or peering curiously out of windows. The moon was almost full but dark banks of heavy rain clouds scudded across the sky making the flashing blue light on the patrol car even more obvious. The spectators were a silent bunch, huddled in twos and threes, cardigans pulled tightly around them against the chill. All that could be heard as Detective Chief Inspector Roper approached the house was the barking of a dog in someone's back garden and the static crackle of the radio receiver pinned to the lapel of the young PC who stood on guard at the door.

'In here, sir,' he said, indicating a closed door to the right of the hallway. A second constable appeared from the nether regions of the house. It was he who actually opened that door.

The smell was what hit them first. The slightly sweet aroma of human flesh beginning to putrify. Then they noticed the body.

On the floor, between the settee and the fireplace, lay the remains of Julia Henderson. One leg was bent beneath her. Trying not to gulp for air, the meal he had eaten before he took Mark out undecided as to whether or not to make a reappearance, Ian Roper gripped the back of an armchair and tried to pull himself together. He did not want to show himself up in front of his subordinates. He was used to the sight of death, but it never ceased to nauseate him. Besides, it was not usually as ugly as this. The last occasion was a simple shooting. One clean bullet hole, very little blood. This was an entirely different matter.

He made a quick assessment of the situation. The fact that the woman had been murdered was not open to doubt. Suicides do not beat their own brains out and there was far too much damage to the head for it to have been a domestic accident. On the carpet were large, dark brown stains, dried and crusty where the blood had dried. Apart from this the room appeared to be undisturbed.

'SOC been notified?' the Chief asked, knowing he would have been but wanting to break the awful silence. His tone was abrupt as he fought down another mouthful of bile, imagining what both the Scene-of-Crime Officer, to whom he had just referred, and the police surgeon had in front of them.

'He's on his way, sir. Doc Harris . . . I mean.'

'It's all right, constable.' Ian knew he meant the police surgeon. Everyone, no matter what their rank, called him Doc Harris.

'He's already here.'

'Here?' Why wasn't he examining the body then?

'Yes, but he said he'd wait until you arrived before he had a proper look. I mean, she's, well, she's obviously dead.' There was no doubt about that.

Sergeant William Baker left the room without being dismissed and stood on the front step, gratefully breathing in the damp evening air, his hypochondriacal fear of chills and bronchitis for once forgotten. The sight of blood he could stomach, but, oh dear, the smell!

The Chief and the PC who showed him in also returned to the hall, shutting the door on a sight they both hoped they would never have to witness again. Each tried to convey the impression that it was all in a day's work, that he was unaffected. Sometimes this sort of pretence was the only thing which helped them survive such situations.

'Who discovered the body?' the Chief asked quietly, the presence of death very much with him.

'I did, sir.'

'And you are?' He was annoyed. He should not have to ask. He thought he knew all his men by name.

'PC Jackson, sir.'

'Tell me about it.'

Jackson flipped open his notebook. Although the recent events were clearly and for ever imprinted in his mind he did not want to make a mistake in front of the boss.

'At seven thirty this evening a neighbour of the deceased telephoned the station. She said she was concerned about Mrs Henderson. It seems there was an arrangement for her to have dinner yesterday evening with the Claytons, that's the neighbours who rang us, sir. Mrs Ann Clayton,' Jackson added, looking up from his notes. Ian nodded. He would let the man tell it his own way, his police terminology and pedantic style of speaking were covering up what he really felt. And he had been the first on the scene, not a pleasant start to a back shift.

'Well, Mrs Henderson didn't show up for the dinner. Oh.' Ian glanced in the direction PC Jackson's gaze had turned. Behind him stood Doc Harris.

'Sorry to interrupt you. I had a quick look, she's dead all right and has been for some time. I thought it best not to do too much until you arrived. I was just having a fag round the back.' Even ageing doctors had their weak spots. Doc Harris had indeed inspected the body but needed a few minutes alone before he was able to perform what was required of him. 'It's a long time since we've had one like this. At least it's clear cut, no question of anything other than murder. Do you want me to carry on or shall I wait for John?' John Cotton was head of the Scene-of-Crime outfit and one of the best at his job. It could be that even the slightest movement of the body might destroy some minute particle of evidence that would only be recognized by John. 'He won't be long, you may as well wait.'

'Okay, son, carry on.' The Chief was addressing PC Jackson.

The man in question continued. 'The Claytons thought she had simply forgotten, so last night Mr Clayton walked over to remind her, but there was no answer. Although it wasn't dark the downstairs curtains were drawn and, as far as he can recall, no lights were showing anywhere in the house. He then assumed she had forgotten and gone out somewhere else. Later he wondered if she was ill in bed. He and his wife were disappointed, they'd gone to a lot of trouble with the meal, and they were also annoyed as she hadn't let them know. They were puzzled too, though, as they felt Mrs Henderson was not the type to forget something like that or be deliberately rude and just not turn up.'

'The meal was arranged for yesterday evening.' It was not really a question, simply the way the Chief put his ideas in order.

'Yes, sir. They thought no more about it until this evening. They were returning from an early drink at the Feathers and noticed the curtains were still drawn and there was no sign of life. It was only at that point it occurred to Mrs Clayton that the house might have been like that for several days. It was then she was really concerned and thought Mrs Henderson must be ill as she hadn't mentioned going away anywhere.'

'What time did the Claytons leave the Feathers?'

PC Jackson consulted his notes again. 'About six thirty.'

'And they didn't ring the station until half past seven.' Again, these words were not interrogative, but Jackson was taking no chances.

'Yes, sir. They weren't certain what to do. Mr Clayton went over and knocked at the door again, but they didn't want to seem interfering, you see.'

The Chief did see. Nowadays it happened so often. People were either afraid to get involved or did not want to appear nosy. That was the trouble with these new housing estates, he thought, because everyone was out at work to pay for their mortgages, old-fashioned neighbourliness had disappeared.

'Is that it?'

'Well,' Jackson continued, 'this might be of some help. The Claytons knew Mrs Henderson worked from home and kept odd hours. She could please herself what time she got up and went to bed. If she worked late into the night she might lie in until ten or ten thirty.' Chance would be the thing the Chief reflected.

'Um. What happened next?'

'When the call came through Frank...I mean PC Stone and me were in the nearest patrol car so we came to have a look. It was as they said, the curtains were drawn and we couldn't get an answer. The back door was unlocked, though, but not open. There were no signs of forcible entry and then, well...'

'Thank you, Jackson, that's fine, you've done a good job.' A greenish pallor was creeping into the young man's face. Ian knew it was time to give him a break.

As if on cue a car pulled up outside, closely followed by a second. The first contained the Scene-of-Crime Officer, John Cotton, an old friend of the Chief's. He strolled confidently into the house.

'Hello, Ian. Anything been touched?'

'No. We're in luck. It was one of my men who found the body.' That, at least, would make his task easier. So often things were moved, or removed, or touched, obliterating clues. 'Everything's just as it was.'

Without displaying the slightest sign of concern, John Cotton opened the door of the lounge, did not hesitate as a draught of foetid air assailed his nostrils and, closing the door behind him, settled down to begin the painstaking task of gathering what evidence he could. Ian left him to it, not in the least envious of his job.

'Now,' he said to Jackson and Stone who were waiting in the hallway for instructions, 'do we know the next of kin? We'll have to notify them before we begin house to house inquiries.' It would not do, as had happened on one occasion, to start asking questions of some little old lady down the road only to discover she was the victim's mother.

'Not yet, sir,' PC Stone replied, 'but Mrs Henderson's handbag's on the kitchen table. We haven't looked in it yet as we didn't want to touch anything,' he added, unnecessarily defensive. It was, after all, correct procedure.

Stone was sent to collect rubber gloves and plastic bags from the SOC. Before he returned, Detective Sergeant Swan and WPC Robbins stepped into the house. They had arrived in the second car.

Barry Swan's promotion was recent and he could not believe his luck at being on duty at the beginning of this case. From what he had heard through the efficient grapevine down at the station he knew this was no accidental death. He also knew it was the solving of a murder which helped the Chief get where he was. If he could prove himself here, maybe he would get his foot up another rung of the promotional ladder quicker than he had anticipated. In his eagerness to do just that he took the initiative of interrupting Judy Robbins, hard at work typing reports, and bringing her along in case female relatives or friends needed comforting.

Judy resented the interruption. She believed if she was supposed to be capable of doing what Barry Swan termed a man's work, he should be equally capable of dealing with bereaved females. She had told him so in no uncertain terms during their short drive to Churchill Way, giving him her final opinion of him, and men like him, before they got out of the car. Barry was already wondering whether it was such a good idea to have brought her.

They were quickly briefed. The information to hand so far was little enough. Then, wearing the gloves PC Stone handed him, the Chief emptied the contents of Julia Henderson's handbag on to the kitchen table. Each item would be individually bagged and labelled, but that was a job for a PC. For now, Ian was content to glance through her diary. At the back was a list of names and addresses and telephone numbers. No Henderson was listed, neither was there any indication of the relationship of the owners of these names to the dead woman.

To the chagrin of Detective Sergeant Swan, it was the plump, dark-haired Judy Robbins who came up with a suggestion.

'Sir, it might not follow, but when I transfer things from one diary to another I always put the most im-

portant names first, you know, family before friends.'
The Chief grunted an acknowledgement. Susan and
Michael Barfoot's number was at the top of the list.
And if they were who he thought they were, he had
only met them recently.

'The name Barfoot mean anything to you?'

'Barfoot? The vicar at St Luke's is called Barfoot.'
Barry raised an eyebrow. So Miss Clever Clogs was
religious as well as being a women's libber. Another bit
of ammunition to be stored away, Ian was thinking,
trying to picture the faces of the Barfoots, but failing.
Names he was good on, faces escaped him. Barry
Swan gave Judy a look, one which she could not fail
to interpret. It made her blush. Judy was aware he did
not like her much, and that feeling was definitely mutual. She had seen him preening himself in front of the
mirror in the canteen, and although she had to admit
he was good looking, his type of looks did not appeal
to her. She preferred her men taller and less pernick-
ety about their appearance. And, in her eyes worse, he
was arrogant and a male chauvinist.

Still wearing the gloves, Ian Roper picked up the
telephone and dialled the Barfoots' number. No point
in traipsing over there if no one was in. The call was
answered on the fifth ring. Michael gave the number
and his name.

'Good evening, sir, I'm Ian Roper, Detective Chief
Inspector here at Rickenham. Are you by any chance
the vicar at St Luke's? Ah, yes, good.' Ian winked at
Judy. 'I wonder if it would be possible for myself and
a colleague to call in and have a chat about a case
we're investigating?' There was a pause as Michael
said he would be pleased to help if he could. 'Thank

you. And this, I take it, is the vicarage number? Fine. Well, if it's convenient to you, sir, we'll be there in about ten minutes.' He hung up. It cost nothing to be polite, at least to start with. Any problems and he would not hesitate to use strong arm tactics, but it was always better to keep on the right side of people for as long as possible.

'Right. Judy, you come with me. Barry, you stay here until everything's tidied up. See you later.' No one would be going home on time that evening.

Barry watched them go, recognizing the signs. He knew the Chief was winding himself up for the case. When he first came to Rickenham Green, Sergeant Baker, easily distinguished as an old hand who knew the score on superior officers, told him that the boss reverted to first names when he was keyed up and ready for action. William Baker was not sure of the motives behind this but guessed it might be a deliberate ploy, a way of making them feel part of a team, encouraging them to go all out in their efforts. Barry was glad he was not going to the vicarage. He prefered to avoid anything connected with religion, and thought churches to be cold, depressing places, reminding him of his own mortality. He could not understand how people attended them out of choice, much less visited them as places of beauty and interest. He also dreaded the first time he had to break the news of a death, which he hoped would not be this evening. For reasons not of his own making the chore had not yet fallen to him. Besides, someone responsible had to stay until the mortuary van came to take the body away, and while he did so he might be able to pick up some vital information. Incredible as it seemed, Julia's body, so obviously lifeless, could not be removed until the doctor officially pronounced her dead.

John Cotton finished his business in the lounge. He was a meticulous man and worked in a slowly increasing radius away from the body. The fewer size ten boots tramping around the place, the better. He stood next to Barry and shook his head. 'Nothing in there to go on, we'll have to wait for the fingerprints. No sign of a weapon, nothing, and what surprises me is that for a murder this violent, there's no sign of a struggle. Come on, we'll start on the rest of the house.' Before they did so Barry's curiosity had to be satisfied. He opened the lounge door and peered in. He wished he hadn't. What he saw made a night alone in the crypt of a church seem like a picnic.

PC Jackson was sent out to make an initial search of the back garden with the aid of a powerful torch, the arc lamps not yet having arrived. Doc Harris verified his initial guess that Julia Henderson was killed sometime between Saturday and Sunday. It was now Wednesday. For the moment he could not be more accurate. The weather on Saturday was much as today, Sunday and Monday were warm, yet Julia's central heating had come on whilst he was examining her. The weather and the heating combined made his task more difficult, but if, as he suspected, she was killed, say, between Saturday night and Sunday morning, she would not have got around to switching it off. PC Stone was instructed to remain at the front of the house. With the advent of the other cars the crowd outside had grown and become less concerned with propriety. A few of them were actually standing on the small patch of unfenced grass which masqueraded as a front garden. It was Stone's job to keep the ghouls away and to ensure they encroached no further.

Barry Swan, John Cotton and Sergeant Baker, armed with gloves and bags, began the painstaking task of going through Julia's belongings.

'I'll start in the bathroom,' John Cotton said, 'it's amazing how much you can learn about someone from the contents of their medicine cabinet. You take the main bedroom.'

Doc Harris went out to his Jaguar, unrecognized by the Chief because it was a new possession, and although it was quite a few years old, one of which he was proud. He lit another cigarette and pondered over his golfing handicap while he waited for the mortuary van.

LESS THAN TEN MINUTES after leaving Churchill Way, Ian Roper and Judy Robbins pulled into the vicarage driveway, tyres scrunching on the gravel semicircle in front of the house. The springlike weather of the last couple of days deceived them, summer was still weeks away. The air was damp and misty and a fine drizzle clung to their clothes, chilling them as they left the warmth of the car and approached the front door. Ian pulled the fleece collar of his well-worn jacket up around his ears and rubbed his hands together, a gesture Judy knew of old. It was a habit rather than a way of getting warm, his way of saying, 'right, let's get on with it'. The Chief, now, was someone Judy did like. In his presence she felt secure and comfortable, his manner always reassuring even when they were in potentially dangerous situations, and he had the ability of hauling his colleagues over the coals, if necessary, without rubbing them up the wrong way. A sense of fairness and a measure of tact predominated all he said and did. She wondered if he treated his wife and son as well as he treated his staff. On the few occasions she had run into Moira she appeared serene and content, so he probably did.

Not short herself, Judy only reached Ian's shoulder in flat shoes, and as they waited for the door to be answered she glanced up at him. She was close enough to notice the tell-tale lines of worry creasing his forehead. They were not visible a few years ago but, she reflected with a wry grin, he had possessed a little more hair then. An outside light came on directly over their heads and Michael Barfoot opened the door. He looked startled.

'Good evening.' Ian extended his hand and was about to introduce himself and Judy, unsure if the man would remember him from amongst all the other wedding guests.

'Chief Inspector Roper. I was expecting you. The name rang a bell when you telephoned. Life is full of coincidences, isn't it? I meet you for the first time on Saturday and here you are again. It was quite a do, wasn't it? I'm sorry, please come in, it's not very pleasant out there tonight.' Michael stood aside to let them in, then led the way down a wide, quarry-tiled hall, spotlessly clean, and showed them into the sitting-room, the room he and Susan used when they were not entertaining. It was more comfortable than the larger, rather formal room across the hall which also served as Michael's office.

He waved a hand at the deep, cushioned armchairs either side of the fireplace. 'Do sit down.'

'This is WPC Robbins,' Ian said before they did so. Michael returned to the settee after switching off the television set which he'd been watching before their arrival.

'Now, how can I help you?'

'I believe you know a Mrs Julia Henderson?'

'Yes, my wife and I know her well, we've been friends for years, ever since she moved here, in fact, about six years ago. She was at the wedding on Saturday. You may have met her yourself.'

It was possible, but there were over two hundred guests, and as for recognizing her, well, that was now out of the question. More coincidences, Ian thought. First the Reverend Barfoot, then the victim herself. It was unnerving to think he'd been in the same room with her only four days ago and now she was dead.

'No, I don't think I did. We didn't stay very long. My wife knows Laura Sutcliffe through some charity work they do together.' Ian smiled apologetically, 'I think our invitation was an act of charity, sort of "let's give our local, overworked Chief Inspector and his good lady a night out". We didn't go to the service, only the reception.'

'No, there were far too many people to fit into the church, I believe there were over three hundred guests at various times. However, if you had met Julia you would certainly have remembered. She's an amazingly beautiful woman. So what's the problem, has she run into the back of someone?' Michael smiled hesitantly. Despite Julia's unwarranted reputation, the idea of her being in trouble with the police was inconceivable. Yet the matter must be serious to bring such a senior officer to his door.

The Chief cleared his throat again. It was obvious that the Reverend thought well of Mrs Henderson. This was one of the worst aspects of the job and there were no words to make it any easier.

'No, sir, something far more serious than that. I'm sorry to have to tell you this, but Mrs Henderson is dead.'

'Dead? Julia? She can't be.' The reaction was almost always the same. No one ever thought someone they knew would die before their time.

'What do you mean, she's dead? Has she had an accident? Oh, God, whatever happened?' Michael's face was white, as the truth began to sink in.

'We have good reason to believe it was not an accident, sir. We are treating the incident as a suspicious death.' At that moment Ian hated himself for having to use well-worn cliches, for having to give such information by way of formal police jargon, but he suspected he would not be able to do it any other way if he had the choice.

'You mean suicide? Not Julia, she would never . . . you don't mean? Oh no. It can't be.' Michael's body drooped forward as if the weight of his torso was too much to bear. Grief showed plainly in his face. Who could possibly want to harm Julia?

'I apologize if I sounded brutal, sir, but there's no pleasant way to put these things. Do you keep any brandy in the house?' Michael nodded, unable to speak, and pointed to the sideboard. He and Susan mostly drank wine but there was usually a bottle or two of spirits left over from Christmas. Ian went to investigate, wondering if Michael Barfoot's reaction was not a bit over the top for someone who was only a friend. He did not know then that Michael treated friendship with much more care and consideration than most and that the effect of the news on his wife was troubling him.

Ian found a bottle with a couple of inches of brandy remaining and, unable to find a suitable glass, poured most of it into a tumbler. Michael's hand trembled as he accepted the glass but after a sip or two he seemed to regain his composure.

'Do you have any idea who might have done it?'

'No, not yet. But we're working on it. We'll find out eventually.' More clichés, but this time Ian was grateful for them. He could hardly say they had absolutely nothing to go on. 'At the moment my main concern is to contact the next of kin. We thought you might be able to help us there.'

Michael frowned. 'As far as I know she didn't have any. Both her parents are dead. They had her late in life and she was an only child.' He paused, trying to remember if Julia ever mentioned anyone else, a distant cousin, maybe. He was unaware he'd already adopted the past tense when referring to her. 'There's her husband, of course.' Ian and Judy exchanged a look. This was the first they knew of any husband. Neither of the Claytons mentioned his existence and they'd only expected Mrs Henderson for dinner. And there was no sign of male habitation at 2 Churchill Way.

'She hardly ever saw him, though,' Michael continued, aware of their surprise. 'They separated about six years ago, that's why Julia moved here, to make a new start. Then she put in for a divorce. She talked to us about it quite a lot at the time, said she wanted to be certain she was doing the right thing, she wanted to be sure the marriage was definitely a mistake before she consulted a solicitor. It was a difficult time for her, she was fond of him, but she felt that wasn't enough. Bart, that's the husband, wouldn't agree to the divorce so she decided to wait the five years. That wasn't a problem for her. She said many times she would never marry again, and she thought it would give Bart the chance to get used to the idea. Apparently he idolized her.'

'So she was still married when she died?' Judy prompted.

'That's strange you should ask. I'm not sure. The decree nisi came through, I know, so it's about now the whole thing should have become final, but I can't say for sure whether she's, was, I mean, still married. But I think Julia would've told us if she'd got her absolute.' Michael shook his head. 'No, really, apart from Bart there's no one. As you probably know, her first husband is no longer alive, he died in a car accident. I don't think Julia ever really got over his death. Oh dear God, Susan will be heartbroken.'

Present husband? First husband? Susan? Ah, yes, Reverend Barfoot's pretty wife. Ian certainly recalled her face. But the cast was growing by the minute.

They would have to make inquiries about the death of husband number one. There could be some connection.

'Susan, your wife, is she here at the moment?' Michael looked up. Already there were dark smudges appearing under his eyes, contrasting with the pallor of his face. Ian was about to do the decent thing and offer to tell her himself. He was greatly relieved to hear she was out at her evening classes.

'Just one last question, Mr Barfoot. Do you know where Bart Henderson lives now?'

'Yes, Saxborough. Or at least he did the last time Julia mentioned him, but I'm afraid I don't know the exact address. It's easy enough to remember because it was another of those coincidences. Julia moved to Rickenham from Saxborough and that was where both Susan and myself went to university. A further coincidence is that Bart is a tutor there.'

'So you knew him?'

'Oh no. We never met him, he wasn't appointed until several years after we left.'

'Dad?' Michael was startled. Temporarily he had forgotten the existence of his children.

'Josh? Aren't you asleep yet?'

Ten-year-old Joshua Barfoot stood in the doorway in his striped pyjamas, a look of open curiosity on his scrubbed face. He had heard the knock on the door and finally could not resist coming down to see who was visiting. On several occasions the appearance of a blond, angelic ten year old in his nightclothes had been rewarded with fifty pence, or even a pound. He was out of luck tonight.

'No, I wasn't asleep.' Josh wondered what was going on. His brother was still up, in the spare room fiddling with the computer which he and Matthew received as a joint Christmas present, but he hadn't come downstairs which was unusual because Matthew's curiosity was greater than his own. But then, he couldn't understand his brother at all lately, he was so moody, and he'd even caught him crying once but knew better than to say anything. He did not want to risk a clip round the ear. However, this was all very exciting. He could not remember ever seeing a police-woman actually in their sitting-room before. He guessed the man with her was a plain clothes detec-tive. Then a terrible thought struck him.

'Dad? Is Mum...?'

'No, Josh,' Michael quickly assured him, 'noth-ing's happened to Mum.' He saw how the scene might appear to his son and went across to ruffle his hair. 'The police are here about something else, nothing for you to worry about. Come on, I'll take you up.' He turned and, amid protestations from Josh who wanted to stay and listen, made his excuses and said he would only be a minute.

'Well, well. Cherchez the husband?' Judy cynically wondered aloud when they were alone. She could quote the statistics on how many murders were com-mitted by someone close to the victim.

'Perhaps,' she continued, 'he decided if he couldn't have her no one else would either. She would be a sin-gle woman again.' It sounded weak even to her own ears.

'Um,' the Chief grunted, equally thoughtful, 'I don't know. Seems a bit too neat somehow. A bit too obvious. He'd have done it sooner I'd have thought. Still, I'll have a chat with him myself, gauge his reac-tion to the news, but it might mean treading on the toes of the Saxborough lot. I'll have to give Harry Watkins a ring. I'm sure he'll co-operate.'

Harry was another old friend of Ian's. They had trained together at Hendon and for some years worked together. As they gained their respective promotions they moved to different areas but always kept in touch. Harry Watkins was now based in Saxborough, which was useful, as he owed Ian a favour.

'I haven't told him anything,' Michael said when he returned a few minutes later. 'But what about Susan? I can tell her, can't I?'

Ian had been about to tell her himself if she was at home so he could hardly refuse the request and if, as the Reverend said, his wife was Mrs Henderson's best friend, she had a right to know before some gossiping neighbour informed her.

'Yes. You can tell her, but would you ask her not to discuss it with anyone until we've had a chat with her?' He knew how soon it would be public knowledge. Most of Churchill Way had been out to witness the arrival of the police and there would be no doubt in their minds with the arrival of the mortuary van, and he'd have to make a brief statement to the press to-night before they got hold of the wrong end of the stick.

'Thank you for your help, sir. I'm sorry we were the bearers of such bad news. Someone will call round in the morning to have a word with your wife. She'll have had time to get used to the idea by then. Meanwhile,' he said, handing Michael a card, 'if you can think of anyone, anyone at all, who might have had a reason to do such a thing, someone who had a grudge, for instance, please give me a ring on this number, or leave a message at the station.' Michael took the card and went with them to the front door.

'I hope you find him soon,' he said as he showed them out.

In the car Judy grinned at the Chief. Despite her earlier comment about the husband, he knew her views on equality. Anyone who worked with her could not help but know. The Chief grinned back when she said, 'They always assume it's a man, don't they?'

MICHAEL SHUT THE DOOR and stood behind it, trembling. It was impossible to accept Julia was dead. Yet she must be. Breathing deeply to steady himself he went up to say good-night to his sons. Josh was already asleep, one arm flung over the side of the bed, but Matthew was still trying to outwit the computer in some space game. 'Come on,' Michael said, 'time for bed.'

'Must I?' He did not look at his father, his body was rigid with an intensity far greater than Michael thought was good for him. He would have to limit the time they spent playing such games. This elder child of his was like a stranger lately.

'You know the rules. School tomorrow, and you've your mock GCSEs coming up.' Matthew switched off the machine and went to his room without saying good-night. Michael was still unused to the surliness displayed recently by this half man, half boy. Hopefully it would pass. Please God.

He went downstairs and lit one grill of the gas fire in the grate. Suddenly he felt very cold. He sat down and remained in the chair, motionless, until Susan returned. His sense of guilt was overpowering. It was as if his prurient thoughts of Julia were somehow responsible for her death.

Wednesday was the one evening during the week Susan had time to herself. Her days were otherwise filled with meetings, church and the Youth Club. Much of this business was conducted at the vicarage and on those occasions she provided coffee and sandwiches, always managing to stretch the budget well beyond what Michael thought possible. And of course there were the boys who still needed a fair bit of attention. Only rarely did they have a night out together although there were plenty of offers to babysit. Matthew and Josh were good kids and all credit was due to Susan. She brought them up to be polite and well behaved without quelling their natural exuberance.

It was a creative writing class Susan attended on Wednesdays. If the tutor praised one of her pieces her face was alight with pleasure. Tonight her pleasure would be short-lived.

The sound of the car in the driveway pulled him out of his reverie and he got up to switch on the outside light. One day, he promised himself, he would get round to putting it on a timeswitch. Opening the door he watched Susan walk jauntily towards him and felt a rush of tenderness. What would this do to her? But he could not protect her from it, better the news should come from him rather than someone else in the morning.

Immediately, she saw from his face something was wrong.

'Michael, what is it? The boys...' She pushed past him, already on the fourth stair before he caught her arm.

'No. No, it's not the boys. They're quite safe. Come on in here and sit down.' Without loosening his grip he led her through to the sitting-room. 'I don't know how to put this,' he began, knowing how the Detective Inspector must have felt. Sensing her agitation he made her sit while he did as that Detective Inspector had done for him and poured out what remained of the brandy. He waited until she took a sip before he spoke.

At first Michael thought she did not understand or that what he said had not sunk in. Susan said nothing, merely took another sip of her drink. Then, without warning, she began to shake from head to foot, her face ashen. Michael removed the glass from her hand before she dropped it. He placed it on the table and wrapped his arms tightly round her, rocking her body against his own, trying to lessen the shock.

She went rigid in his embrace.

'When?' she asked through gritted teeth. 'When did they say it happened?' It was an odd thing to ask, not how, but when?

'They didn't say.'

'And you didn't think to find out, I suppose.' Michael found her reaction far from relevant, but he was not taken aback by her anger. He had witnessed enough bereavements through his work to know that grief took many forms. The range of emotions was wide. He shook his head and continued holding her hand wondering how long it would be before she was able to cry.

Susan was cold. Despite the heating and the gas fire her hands were freezing. She did not trust herself to unclench her teeth, it was the only way she could prevent the spasms of shuddering which washed over her. Michael was aware of the self control she was exerting and was proud of her but he also sensed the shock had gone deeper than she knew. Perhaps it was to be expected. She and Julia were so very close. Although Susan was immensely popular—everyone spoke highly of the vicar's lovely young wife—Julia was her only real friend.

It was a long time before Susan began to cry, her initial tears turning to sobs. Michael saw then there would be no need to call out the local GP to give her something to see her through the night. 'It's awful,' she gulped, 'poor, poor Julia. Oh, Michael, what will I do without her?' There was no answer he could make.

Gradually she became calmer and eventually gave him a wan smile and said she was all right. She stood up, brushed down her skirt and went out into the kitchen where she immediately began taking the ornamental dishes from the top of the dresser and piled them into a bowl of hot, soapy water. She scrubbed at them as if her own life depended on it.

Michael sighed but left her to it. Long ago he had learned that scrubbing and polishing was his wife's way of ridding herself of unwanted emotions. It was not the first time he had had to stand back and watch. Always house-proud, Susan, when upset, would take it to extremes.

THREE

WHEN BARRY SWAN returned to the station it was after ten thirty and he was frustrated because he had little new to report. What exactly he hoped to learn by staying at Churchill Way was uncertain. If the experts failed it was not likely he would succeed. It was now recorded that Julia Henderson had been dead for several days, but that was obvious to all concerned before Doctor Harris confirmed it. All the routine procedures were followed faithfully without, so far, any further light being thrown upon the situation. The results of the post mortem would provide more accurate details.

There was little the Chief could do until morning. All the officers involved were debriefed in the incident room but the identity of Mrs Henderson's killer remained a mystery. He abandoned the idea of instigating house to house inquiries tonight. It was not as if the murder was recent; besides, they would prove useless at this hour. People would be tired, or already in bed and annoyed at being disturbed, or, if they spent the evening at the pub it was likely their observations would be more reliable in the morning.

After leaving the vicarage Ian and Judy returned briefly to the scene of the crime and, certain nothing was being left to chance, drove back to the station. Ian put through a call to Harry Watkins at Saxborough but learned he had left work early to take his wife to a

dinner and dance, something Ian knew he should do
more often himself. He hesitated after he replaced the
receiver, speculating whether he could get away with
doing nothing about Bart Henderson until he spoke to
Harry personally. His sense of duty prevailed. It had
been a selfish thought, he was in charge of the case,
true, but could not hope to interview every suspect
himself. Besides, whether or not the man still loved his
wife, he had a right to know immediately. And if he
was guilty of her murder the sooner he was seen the
quicker they might get a confession. Yet despite the
lack of evidence pointing elsewhere, or anywhere at
all, Ian did not feel the man was guilty. It was an in-
expressible feeling and he knew he must not let it influence his objectivity.

'Coffee. No sugar.' Judy Robbins put a squishy,
polystyrene container on the desk in front of him. No
matter which button was depressed on the vending
machine which stood in the corridor it always dis-
pensed a sludgy, brown liquid which passed for tea,
coffee or oxtail soup. Ian sighed and steeled himself to
take a sip. Bad enough having to drink the stuff, but
without sugar? Blast Moira and her healthy eating.
However, on this occasion Judy might be right, the
contents of the container had a certain coffee-ish
aroma.

'We may as well call it a night,' he decided after a
few more sips. It had been a long day, especially for
Judy whose shift officially ended a couple of hours
ago. It was hard to remember not to take her for
granted at times. She was between boyfriends and had
no commitments beyond the job. There were many
occasions when she stayed on to help rather than re-

turn to an empty flat even when there were cuts on overtime.

'OK,' Ian addressed the half dozen people sitting disconsolately around him, 'we've done all we can to-night but I want you all here early tomorrow.' This was added for the benefit of Barry Swan who was not re-nowned for his punctuality. Tomorrow would not be a problem; the young detective would be up at the crack of dawn if necessary. He was determined to prove himself on this case. 'Eight o'clock,' Ian said, making meaningful eye contact with Barry.

He left the building and headed towards the car-park. Ian was tired, very tired, but thanks to Brian Lord, realized the cause was mostly the stress of the past four hours or so. He had seen the same look on the faces of his detectives. Once the initial excitement was over they knew what a long, hard slog was to fol-low; the endless interviews, the repetition of the ques-tions, dead end inquiries and false trails. Only when the case was concluded would they celebrate. Murder was a thing senior officers both loved and dreaded. It was an inquiry they could get their teeth into, which kept them on their toes and made the blood circulate faster, but all the time at the back of their minds was the nagging fear that this might be the case which re-mained on the books unsolved.

So far, Ian thought as he drove towards Belmont Terrace, only the bare minimum had been achieved. The next of kin was established and informed, unfor-tunately without his own presence, the time of death was known, albeit roughly, and an incident room was set up. And there, he reflected grimly, was the not very impressive list of their achievements.

As Harry Watkins was not expected home until very late, Ian had to make do with a promise from a Detective Sergeant at Saxborough that Bart Henderson would be seen that night and a detailed report of the interview faxed through to him at Rickenham. The man was as good as his word and several pages of information were now to hand. Ian mulled over their contents as he drove home.

Ian put his key in the lock and opened the door as quietly as he could. Moira and Mark were probably sound asleep by now. He was surprised to see a light shining under the door of the front room. Perhaps she was watching a late film. He hoped it was not to give him an earful about dropping Mark off early. He placed his briefcase under the telephone table in the hall and his car keys on top and, brushing back his hair with a tired gesture, went to face the music.

'Hello, love. You needn't have waited up.'

'What happened, Ian? What was it this time?'

'Oh, Moira, not now. Please. It's been one hell of a night.'

'I know. That is I know you wouldn't have been called away from the football unless it was a major problem, but when I went up to see Mark earlier, he was crying. He's fourteen years old and in tears because he needs a father. And before you say anything, I know how much the job means and that you warned me years ago how it would be. I know that, but Mark doesn't. Talk to him tomorrow will you, please?'

Ian put a hand on her head. 'I will, I can promise you that much. And I know what a pig I've been. I only realized once we were at the match that Mark would much rather have gone somewhere else.' It was true. Seeing his son's unenthusiastic face he recalled the conversation which took place when he first went to the comprehensive school. Like all the new boys he was tried out for the soccer team and despite assurances he was good enough for the under twelves Mark insisted someone else be chosen. He would, he told his games teacher, and later his parents, play in school time, when it was compulsory, but for his extra-curriculur activity he opted for chess. On that day Ian's hopes of ever seeing his own son play at Carrow Road were dashed for ever.

'All I can say is that I'm sorry. But I did do something right today, I ate the sandwiches you prepared and kept away from the canteen.' Moira smiled, she saw he was trying to make up for Mark's disappointment. Aware of the quality of the canteen food, and her husband's expanding waistline which a diet of pies and chips did nothing to aid, she had started to give him a packed lunch. She was aware that sometimes it probably went in the bin and that Ian ate with his colleagues; she could always tell by his clothes, the smell of grease seeped into them. But to give him his due he had lost a few pounds.

'Are you hungry now?'

'No.' He saw her surprised expression. 'I'm not just saying that because I don't want to put you to any trouble, it's just after tonight, well, I couldn't face anything.'

She had not asked but this was her cue.

'Yes, what exactly was it that took you away from the match?'

'A murder. A woman called . . .'

'A murder? Here in town?' Moira was suitably shocked.

'Julia Henderson. Ever heard of her?'

Moira thought for a moment. The name meant nothing. 'She was at the wedding on Saturday. You didn't come across her then?' She shook her head.

'No, I would have remembered. I only spoke to the Barfoots and Laura and that rogue of a husband of hers, and there were so many people.' She did not add that they had had to leave early because Ian had had a busy week and was tired. Mark was spending the night with a friend.

They had a cup of tea and Ian told her as much as he knew about the case. Moira did not need to be told that she must discuss it with no one. Not once during their years together had she broken a confidence.

In bed, not long after, Ian impatiently brushed Moira's hand away when she placed it on his thigh as they lay silently side by side. His brain was overactive, he needed to wind down a bit more and knew he had come to bed too soon after leaving work. He thought about all the problems. There were too many unsolved cases, not one of national importance, until tonight that was, but a whole list of petty crimes and that list was growing daily. With a murder investigation under way the list was likely to double before they could turn their attention to it. He couldn't understand it. Was it simply that more offences were being committed? Was society responsible, the old theory about a decline in moral standards? They discussed the possibilities down at the station but Ian felt it was too much of an intellectual exercise for this time of night. Perhaps, he consoled himself, it was simply a case of understaffing. Or were the criminals becoming more competent?

He smiled grimly to himself at this idea. No, he'd beat the bastards in the end. Realizing his teeth were no longer clenched together he took a deep breath and began the relaxation technique. Parting his lips he let his tongue drop back behind his teeth, as taught by the once dreaded psychologist, then he tightened all the muscles along the length of his body before letting go and trying to make himself feel as if he were sinking through the mattress.

Moira recognized the signs and turned over expecting him to fall asleep. A few moments later she was pleasantly surprised to feel her husband's arm slide around her and his hand rest tentatively on her breast.

'Um,' she whispered, 'all I can say is thank goodness for psychology lecturers,' as Detective Chief Inspector Roper proved he'd learned his lessons well.

SAXBOROUGH'S first attempt to find Bart Henderson was abortive. He had moved from the address given on the Register of Electors and the woman with whom he had lodged since the time of Julia's departure until quite recently had no forwarding address, but he was soon located through the university. The Principal, Julian Wickes, was contacted on his mobile telephone, he, too being at a function. Ian wondered what sort of social whirl the people of Saxborough enjoyed. Everyone seemed to be at a dinner. Mr Wickes gave permission for the police to peruse his personnel file. He was sorry, he did not know the address off hand. Next, the girl who held the keys to the filing cabinet had to be persuaded to accompany them to the university. She apparently was meeting friends at a nightclub at eleven but her unhelpful attitude altered when the patrolmen said they would drop her off there on their way back. 'Doesn't anyone stay in at night over there?' Ian had asked rhetorically when he first scanned the report. Scanned, because although he asked for details he was not expecting the minutiae of the private lives of the inhabitants of Saxborough. However, he finally reached the important part. Bart's new address, and the telephone number accompanying it, was that of a boarding house similar to the one he had left. His finances could run to something better but he chose to live in digs about a mile and a half away from the town centre.

The landlady was most obliging. She informed the two men who appeared on her doorstep that her lodger was not in, but seemed prepared to settle down and answer as many questions as they were prepared to ask.

Yes, she told them, Mr Henderson had been with her for almost a year. 'A real gentleman,' she said, 'quiet. Pays his rent in advance and no nonsense, if you know what I mean.'

'No girlfriends?' the Detective Constable wanted to know. A Chief Inspector required details, details he was going to have.

'None that I've ever seen. And he's not, you know, that way either.' Her interrogators exchanged a glance. It appeared they were dealing with a lady who had difficulty in imparting information in a straightforward manner. Nonetheless they were now in possession of information they had not elicited. No girlfriends might mean nothing. Or it could mean he was obsessed with his wife, or ex-wife, maybe enough to kill her. To the delight of Mrs Roomes, a name which, because of the way she earned a few extra pounds, caused the policemen a secret smile, what she said was being jotted down in a notebook. At last they discovered where they might find Mr Henderson.

'Oh, in the pub on the corner. He's there every night except weekends. He goes away then, he does, stays with friends. Still pays me the full week, though. Wish they was all like him.' She looked at the clock. 'He'll be back any minute. Comes in at a quarter to eleven every night. You could set your watch by him. Why don't you sit down and I'll make you a nice cup of tea?'

They had done just that, according to the report. They did not want to miss him now. If he returned after they left Mrs Roomes was sure to mention their visit and he might do a runner. They had no intention of apprehending him in the pub, they knew too well the effect their appearance would have. And it was not drink drivers they were after—they left that to traffic division—but it might conceivably be a murderer. If he was simply a man about to receive bad news he did not need the added embarrassment of being seen escorted out of his local by the Old Bill.

As they sipped their very indifferent cups of tea they heard Bart Henderson's key in the lock, closely followed by a loud rattling noise and the words 'Oh, shit'. Being observant young men they correctly assumed Mr Henderson, presumably a little under the weather, had taken a tumble into the coat stand in the hall. They asked Mrs Roomes to excuse them. 'We'll see Mr

Henderson in his room if you don't mind. And thanks for the tea.'

Mrs Roomes sniffed, put out that she was not to be a party to the interview, but she could hardly refuse to let them upstairs. She was satisfied it must be to do with those awful students Mr Henderson taught. Drugs most likely.

The two men watched Bart carefully as they imparted the news but it was hard to gauge his reactions with any accuracy as he was undoubtedly drunk. It took him several minutes to get his bearings and only when he searched through his pockets more than once to find his cigarettes and rummaged in a drawer for matches did he seem aware he had visitors.

Bart shook his head. 'Juliashnotdead' was all he said. He was totally bewildered, unsure if there were two men in his room telling him ridiculous things or if his gin-sodden imagination was playing tricks.

One of the men went downstairs and asked Mrs Roomes to provide some black coffee for her lodger. She did so, hovering in the open doorway hoping for an invitation to join them. It was not forthcoming.

It took two mugs of the coffee and much splashing of cold water before Bart was fully able to appreciate what was happening. As it sank in he aged visibly. He sank into the only chair in the room, shoulders hunched in despair, noisy sobs racking his body. He did not possess a handkerchief and a thin stream of mucus hung pitifully from his nose, unnoticed until he looked up at the bearers of the news and felt it against his top lip. Without embarrassment he raised an arm and wiped both nose and mouth in the crook of his tweed-covered elbow.

His grief appeared genuine. It is one of the hardest emotions to fake, but too much alcohol could have the same effect.

Bart answered some questions as to his whereabouts over the past week with as much accuracy as the gins and tonics would allow. Weekdays were easy, both the university and Mrs Roomes would vouch for most of his time and he expressed no objection to them checking his movements with the landlord of the pub. But the weekend posed a problem. He always stayed with friends, of which, apparently, he had many, scattered over the country. He could not for the moment remember where he was last Saturday and Sunday, his mind was too blurred by the alcohol. He thought he might be able to let them know in the morning when he was sober. He did not ask why they wanted to know his movements, even in Bart's state it was obvious. He was being regarded as a suspect.

Although worded in more formal language this was the essence of the faxed report. When Ian read it before leaving the station he knew there was no alternative but to wait until morning to hear Bart's alibi. Just before he drifted off to sleep, his arm around Moira, Ian wondered if the drunkenness was an act, that Bart, if guilty, needed time to find someone to give him an alibi. Now was not the time to think about it, he would only wake himself up again. Tomorrow the hard work would start, the nitty-gritty business of finding out who last saw Mrs Henderson alive. Who were her friends and who were her enemies? He knew she worked from home, the Claytons said as much to PC Jackson. Who employed her? Or was she self-employed? And then there was the prying into her

personal possessions. Death was not usually digni-
fied, murder even less so, but that last task Ian felt to
be positively degrading.

He turned over, removing his arm gently so as not
to disturb Moira. It was no good. He was not able to
sleep. He was over tired and not even the sex had
helped. He got up and went downstairs to make tea,
realizing that he now felt hungry. Opening the fridge
to see if there was anything he fancied in a sandwich
he knocked a saucer off the dish it was covering and
it clattered to the floor. Stepping back quickly to avoid
it hitting his bare foot he knocked over one of the
kitchen chairs and sent it crashing to the ground.
Cursing silently, he picked it up and switched on the
kettle but Moira had heard the noise and come down
to investigate.

'Sorry, love. I was trying to be quiet.'

'Never mind. I'll have some coffee if you're making it.' Ian did not understand how his wife could
drink gallons of the stuff all day long and still sleep as
soundly as she did, when he hadn't woken her, that is.
'Do you want something to eat?' She knew how large
his appetite was and he had not had anything since
lunchtime yesterday.

'I was going to make myself a sandwich.'

'It's all right, I'll do it.' It was quicker, and there
would be less mess. She got out the necessary ingredients and started to butter some bread. It was gra-
nary and Ian was not that keen on it, but he was
getting used to it. He made a pot of tea and poured
boiling water over some instant granules for Moira,
then took the mugs through to the front room. He sat
in the chair Moira had vacated earlier and idly picked

up her book. It was lying face down, pages splayed over the arm of the chair, a habit of hers which irritated him. Books should be treated with respect. Was it such a big deal to use a bookmark and avoid damaging the spine?

At first he could not make out what he was looking at. He flipped casually through the pages, they were covered not only with writing but also some hieroglyphics, then, tired as he was, it dawned on him that what he held in his hand was a copy of *Pitman's Shorthand for Beginners*.

'Moira!' Book in hand, he was in the kitchen in a few strides. Butter-covered knife poised over the bread, she turned and smiled placidly. 'Oh dear. Sorry. I meant to find a bookmark.'

'Never mind the bookmark. Why are you reading this? What on earth do you want to learn shorthand for?' He knew, of course, before he asked, and he tried to keep calm and fight the sinking feeling in his stomach.

'Oh Ian, I told you several weeks ago, when we had that lovely day out, the three of us. Don't you remember? When you promised to spend more time with Mark? And I said what I wanted to do with my life? We both decided on some changes.'

'Yes, I know that. I agreed to this stupid dieting...'

'That was before. We discussed that a long time ago. I'm talking about my own future.'

Ian racked his brains. He hadn't the faintest idea what they talked about that day. Mark, yes, he had agreed to take him out now and again, and he was keeping to his promise to be home early at least one night a week so's they could eat a meal as a family, but he remembered nothing about Pitman's bloody shorthand. His anger was really directed at himself. He knew if it had been an interview, or interrogation with a suspect every word would be etched in his memory until the end of the case. Obviously the same rules did not apply at home.

'I've kept my side of it,' he said defensively, 'with Mark, and in case you've forgotten, I was home Saturday afternoon and evening, and early on Monday, but this...' he waved the book under her nose as if it were one of the obscene publications recently confiscated from under the counter of the newsagent on the corner of Waveney Road.

'Ian,' Moira began reasonably, 'I've spent my whole adult life looking after you and Mark and our home, and your meals have always been on time, even,' she continued, wondering at the wisdom of her next words, 'when you haven't been here to eat them. I'm thirty-five, hardly ancient, I know, but life is passing by. I'm entitled to something of my own. Don't forget I married you straight from college, I've never even had a job.' Seeing his eyes darken she raised a hand as if physically to stop him from speaking. 'I'm not blaming you, don't think that, it was my choice. But my mind is made up. I'm taking a secretarial course which fits in perfectly with Mark's school hours. After all, he's fourteen now, he's hardly a baby. And don't worry, I'll still fit in the housework and cooking. It's just that sometimes I don't think you realize how boring it is being stuck at home. Oh, I know I've got the odd morning at the Oxfam shop, but that's hardly inspiring.'

It was one of the longest speeches Moira had ever made. Without a word in reply Ian walked away. In the front room he poured himself a stiff scotch, looked at the glass and added some more, then took it, and himself, off to bed. 'Boring?' he asked himself. 'She thinks our marriage is boring? She tells me now when this might be the biggest case I've dealt with. The woman's got no consideration. Well, fine. Let her get on with it. It obviously doesn't matter that my son's going to be a latchkey kid and I'll be spending any spare time I'm lucky enough to get in the sodding launderette.' The thought that there would be no more steak and kidney pies, no more stews with dumplings, hurt most. 'Ah,' he decided, 'that's what it's all been about, this dieting lark, she's been weaning me off her cooking.'

Moira wrapped the untouched sandwich in cling-film and put it in the fridge. She would wait until she thought Ian was asleep before joining him in bed. No argument between them had yet been bad enough for one of them to resort to the spare room but she did not want to risk a further row. She was terribly disappointed. When she first mentioned it Ian put up no objections to what she proposed doing, because, she now realized, he had not been listening. It was too late now. She was enrolled on the course and had purchased the necessary books and was looking forward to starting more than she thought possible. Too bad the day had to end this way, but Ian had been very late home. She excused his outburst by putting it down to tiredness or problems at work. He was bound to be more reasonable in the morning.

Moira, in her usual accommodating way, tried to put herself in his place, to exercise the same understanding she had throughout their marriage. She was startled when she found herself shutting the fridge door with a little more strength than was actually required.

'Well bugger it,' she said aloud to the empty kitchen, 'I want to do it and I'm going to do it.'

THE NEXT MORNING the Chief arrived in his office at seven thirty, still in a foul temper. He had got out of bed quietly so as not to disturb Moira and went to the lengths of shaving at the kitchen sink so she would not hear the water running. He did not want to face her just yet. Part of the reason was he believed he was in the wrong; he didn't like to admit that when he first picked up the book he vaguely remembered her saying something about getting a job. And he had not been fair and fairness was a thing he prided himself on. But worse, he hated apologizing, and at some point he would have to do so. For now he was working on the basis that by the time he got home that evening it would all have blown over. He was taking the coward's way out and he knew it. Someone had to pay.

'And where the hell have you been?' he snapped at Barry Swan when he sauntered in at one minute past eight.

Barry glanced at the sensible, old-fashioned clock with large Arabic figures. The minute hand had barely left the twelve.

'Sorry, sir, thought you said eight o'clock.' He was vaguely sarcastic but it was the first indication he had that the boss was not always unflappable.

'Get yourself a coffee, son, I'll have one too, didn't mean to snap,' this was said gruffly and with some difficulty. 'I didn't sleep too well with all this on my mind. Oh, two sugars please.' There, how was that for a bit of rebellion?

Barry went to get the coffee. 'More like a row with the old woman,' he thought as he pressed the buttons.

By eight thirty as many men and women as could be spared were out on the streets beginning the mundane inquiries. But they knew it was these rather than brilliant feats of deduction which usually led to the solving of crimes. Small discrepancies in witnesses' statements, casual slips of the tongue, liars with bad memories, these were the bones of an investigation. These bones were fleshed out with the aid of modern technology. Stomach content analysis, blood types, secretions, computer files of previous similar convictions, such things which could prove beyond a shadow of a doubt that A did not arrive at the restaurant as arranged or B could not have raped his sister and C was already safely behind bars.

But before they reached that stage friends, neighbours and tradesmen had to be interviewed. Before they could employ technology a suspect had to be found.

Detective Sergeant Swan went to see the Claytons in case they remembered anything else which prompted them to contact the police. Ann would not be starting her new job until after the summer holidays and promised to be in during the morning. There was no reason for Gerry not to go to work and he told them he could be contacted in the office of the Morleys' farm. The Chief took it upon himself to meet Susan Barfoot. She, of all people, should be of most help. Women best friends often knew more about each other than did their husbands. He found a free Detective Constable to accompany him in order to take an official statement if necessary.

Ian's briefing to his men was just that, brief. What he wanted was as many details of the dead woman's life as possible; where she shopped, her hairdresser, whether she was on speaking terms with the milkman, anything, anything at all whether or not they thought it had any relevance. He was going to solve this one quickly.

Meanwhile, before he went to the vicarage there was Martyn Bright to speak to. He was not available last night when he rang and he did not like leaving messages on the desk. They were usually misconstrued. He dialled the familiar number.

'Martyn, please, it's Ian Roper.' The girl on the switchboard put him through with no hesitation. When the Chief Inspector rang the *Rickenham Herald* offices voluntarily it meant there was something big on.

'Christ, Ian, is that all you can give me?' Martyn said after Ian read the short, prepared statement. Martyn had taken over the paper a little over a year ago. He was a likeable man, pleasant to have a drink with but when he was in the office he gave Ian the impression of having watched 'Citizen Kane' a few too many times. The six sheets of local news which plopped through letterboxes all over the town once a week were bulked out by many pages of advertising. It was not exactly the ideal medium for a world-wide scoop.

'You know how it is, Martyn. When I've got more I'll give it to you,' Ian replied, falling into the editor's own jargon.

The statement did not give much away. For the moment readers would merely learn that a thirty-six-year-old woman was found dead at her home on Wednesday evening and that the police were treating the incident as a suspicious death. Ian said goodbye before he could be asked anything further.

Temporarily ignoring the Detective Constable who stood beside him impatient to get going, Ian turned his attention to Julia's diary, or rather a copy of the names and addresses it contained. He had already flicked through the individual days but it seemed she either had no appointments or she did not bother to note them down. Perhaps she was one of those people who simply circle dates on a calendar, a most infuriating practice to someone in Ian's position.

Apart from the Barfoots' there were several other local numbers, belonging to her doctor, her dentist and the local branch of one of the big banks, but none that could be deemed as that of a friend. Loose behind the back pages were cards of cab firms and one from a local plumber. It did not necessarily follow she ever used any of them but they needed to be checked. There were several London numbers, central London because of the 071 code. He gave the list to a desk-bound constable and asked him to contact them all. Her doctor would be interviewed later. Doctors were useful, sometimes providing the motive. Julia might have been pregnant and trying to screw the father for money, or suffering from some disease which was infectious. If it was of a sexual nature it might be motive enough for murder. Naturally they would show up in the PM but the family GP knew the person as a whole which was of far greater importance.

Ian noticed it had begun to rain. He pulled his jacket off the peg behind the door, turned to the constable and said, 'Come on then, what're you waiting for?' as he headed for the stairs.

Susan opened the front door of the vicarage and Ian was once more taken aback by her looks. She was a slight, wistfully beautiful blonde, wearing jeans, a man's shirt and a pair of open sandals. For some reason, maybe the way in which she wore them, the clothes added to her femininity. A bucket of steaming water sat on the floor and half of the quarry tiles were gleaming wet. Although interrupted in the middle of this strenuous task, her face was deathly pale.

'Mrs Barfoot? I don't know if you recall, but we met briefly on Saturday. At the wedding.'

'Yes, I do. I was expecting you. Michael told me someone would come. Come in, won't you?' She seemed emotionless and made no reference to the fact they had recently met. She showed them through to the sitting-room and asked if they wanted some coffee. Ian accepted for both of them. He needed a minute or two to let his impressions sink in. For some reason a biblical quotation sprang to mind. He was, he supposed, in the appropriate place for such a thing to happen, but for him it was not a common occurrence. It was damned annoying that he could not recall the exact words—his Sunday School days were too far distant—but the sentiment was there. He jotted the few words he could recall on to a piece of paper and stuffed it into his jacket pocket.

Susan, minus the rubber gloves she was wearing when she opened the door, returned bearing a tray covered with a lace cloth and a jug of fresh coffee. The cups, Ian noted, were bone china. It made a welcome change from chipped mugs and polystyrene beakers.

'You know why I'm here, Mrs Barfoot,' Ian stated gently once they were seated with full cups in front of them. Susan nodded. 'I understand how you must be feeling at the moment, but if we're to find Mrs Henderson's killer quickly, the sooner we know everything about her the better. We need all the help you can give us.'

'She was my only friend.' The irrelevancy was spoken in a low, well-modulated voice which contained a hint of anger rather than the pathos the words suggested. But, like Michael, Ian knew anger was part of the grieving process.

'Yes, your husband told us. Which is why we'd like you to talk about her, to tell us everything you knew about her. Her habits, hobbies, interests, everything. From what I understand, you probably knew her better than anyone else in Rickenham Green. Do you think you feel up to it?'

An hour later the two men returned to the station leaving Susan to refill her bucket and finish cleaning the floor. She had furnished them with a lengthy and what they must assume to be accurate timetable of Julia's life. Nothing in it struck them as being of vital importance but comparisons with other statements might show some discrepancy. The notes were typed and added to the pile of information already accumulating.

Barry Swan was back from seeing the Claytons and had taken over the task of telephoning the numbers in Julia's diary.

'Any good?' Ian mouthed when he saw what he was doing. Barry shrugged and grimaced, gestures which could have meant anything, but which he could not elucidate as the call he was making was answered. The Chief took himself off to the interview room where Barry soon joined him. The information gathered during the morning was already being collated.

Sergeant Baker and a couple of other men spent the early part of the day at 2 Churchill Way which was under twenty-four hour surveillance for the time being. There, they systematically worked their way through Julia's meticulously-filed paperwork and came to the disappointing conclusion there was nothing there to point to a financial grudge. Her bills had been paid on time; electricity, telephone and poll tax receipts were neatly arranged on a prong in date order going back over three years. Amongst these were a few other receipts and corresponding guarantees for goods purchased. Someone as methodical as this would surely not owe personal debts. Her current account cheque was balanced with every transaction and showed there was a sum of £193.60 in the bank.

'Phew,' William Baker said when he opened a Building Society pass book. 'Eleven thousand pounds. That's more like it.' The capital had not been touched for five years and the interest was paid into her current account quarterly. This was not the clue they hoped to find. Later that day it was ascertained Julia and Bart had owned their own properties before they met. Upon their marriage they sold both and bought the house they lived in together. When the marriage broke up Bart sold their home, unable to bear all the reminders, and the balance of the money was divided between them. Julia chose to use only a small percentage of the money as a down payment on Churchill Way and continue to pay a mortgage. She liked the idea of having some savings for the first time in her life and her income, combined with the interest, was enough to live on.

Paying-in books and bank statements showed she received sporadic credits of between three and five hundred pounds which came from Hollinshead and Associates. They were payments from Julia's agent. Pippa Hollinshead's number was one of those listed in her diary and it was soon established that Mrs Henderson wrote freelance articles on modern and antique furnishing for magazines and colour supplements which she sold through the agency. Pippa Hollinshead said if they would like to ring back sometime in the afternoon she could issue them with a list of Julia's work, where and when it was published and the amount she received, less, of course, Ms Hollinshead's commission. She went on to say that Julia had no formal training in antiques and was not considered an expert but she had an eye for arranging a room and her articles appealed to the readers of those magazines.

'Not like those love stories my wife buys,' Sergeant Baker volunteered later when they took a break to eat a calorie-laden meal in the canteen, 'but those expensive monthly ones, so they told me upstairs. All pictures if you ask me. Don't know which is worse.'

Ms Hollinshead agreed to speak to the Metropolitan Police if need be but for now the information she gave was adequate. She was shocked and upset at the manner of Mrs Henderson's death but not distraught. Their relationship was purely on a business level. They rarely met but they were on friendly terms if such an occasion arose.

'Well that's confirmed what the Claytons told us on Wednesday,' Barry said before swallowing a forkful of chips smothered in tomato sauce, 'that she worked from home. I don't think there's much to go on there though.'

'Yes, the Claytons. Haven't had a chance to ask you how you got on there. Find out anything useful?'

'M'notes are upstairs.' Barry indicated upstairs with the prongs of his fork and pushed his plate away. He started on a large slice of strawberry cheesecake the fruit of which was coloured a far more sinister red than any strawberry Ian had ever seen.

BARRY HAD CALLED on Ann first. All she told him matched the statement he later took from her husband. They had moved to Rickenham about a month ago having decided to leave London for a more rural life. Mr Clayton had become cynical and disillusioned about the teaching profession and wanted a complete change. He arrived two weeks before his wife who was working out her notice, which gave him the chance to make a few alterations to the house. When Ann arrived he had just started working for the Morleys. He described himself as a Farm Manager but

admitted his responsibilities were few. He made up the
wages and oversaw the smooth running of the place.
In his opinion it ran smoothly enough without his in-
terference and besides, he knew little about farming.
But Dennis Morley liked the idea of having a manager and the arrangement suited Gerry perfectly.

Ann wanted to leave London as much as her husband and a small country town seemed ideal. She was
offered a post at the local infants school starting after
the summer holidays. But as for Julia Henderson neither of them knew of her existence until two weeks ago
when they met her by chance in the Three Feathers and
struck up a conversation. It was a convivial Sunday
lunch-time. Julia mentioned she went there every week
after church.

'When she first spoke to us I thought she might be
a religious freak or something, trying to drum up
business for the vicar, but that was far from the truth.
She's, was, I mean, a very modern, very confident
lady. In fact, Ann and I went last Sunday. Didn't see
Julia though. We were surprised how full St Luke's
was, must've been thirty people there. Anyway, on
that Sunday we all walked back together and she suggested we have a night out at the local Indian restaurant to give us a break from the decorating. Ann got
on well with her, she was pleased to find someone to
talk to who wasn't a teacher. We saw her the following Sunday in the pub and, as the house is finished,
asked her to come over for a meal to celebrate. That
was this Tuesday, and, as you know, she didn't show
up.'

Barry saw that neither of the Claytons could be of
much assistance in piecing together the last few days

of Julia's life. They did not know her well enough to comment on her routine or who her friends might be.

'How was it then,' Barry wanted to know, 'if you hardly knew her, you were concerned or observant enough to think something was wrong? Something so badly wrong you decided to call us?'

'It's difficult to say really. We're new here and Julia was the first person to make us feel really welcome. You're right, of course, we didn't know her that well but we both got the feeling she was an open, honest person and if there was some reason she couldn't make it that night she would have let us know.'

Ann had said the same thing, adding she thought she and Julia would have become good friends if she'd lived and that, despite her intelligence and good looks, she felt she may have been lonely.

Barry was convinced Ann was telling the truth. She struck him as being straightforward, with no side to her, even if she was a little dowdy. With a bit of effort she would be attractive. But there was something about Gerry Clayton he was not so sure of. He came away with the feeling that a lot was left unsaid.

'And,' Barry told the Chief when they were back in the incident room, 'just like everyone else, the last time they saw her was at the reception at the Country Club on Saturday night.'

By this time every member of the force in Rickenham Green was aware of the wedding. The response to the question, 'When did you last see Mrs Henderson?' was invariably the same. Half the town must have attended.

'Mrs Henderson was still there when the Claytons left at ten thirty.'

'How come they were invited if they've only lived here a few weeks?'

'Through the Morleys, the bride's parents. Dennis Morley told Clayton it would be a good opportunity for them to meet people. He also said he was sick of the whole bloody thing but as he was footing the bill he'd ask who he damned well liked. They didn't attend the church service, just the piss-up afterwards and then they didn't stay late because they didn't want to appear pushy. Apart from the Morleys, the only other person they knew was Mrs Henderson. Oh, and Susan Barfoot. Clayton had bumped into her once or twice in the street.

'I think I'll pay that man another visit. There's something not quite right, something he's not telling. Unless you'd prefer to see him yourself, that is,' he added deferentially. Barry hoped the Chief would refuse because he had a hunch he already knew who the murderer was.

FOUR

ALTHOUGH Julie Henderson's doctor and dentist proved unhelpful as far as information was concerned, by mid-afternoon things began to move. Detective Chief Inspector Roper was confident that the murder took place immediately after the party and as she was one of the last to leave there was a strong possibility one of the guests was responsible. Of course there was an awful lot of interviewing to be got through before any real progress could be made. All the hotel staff, as well as the guests, must be seen. He and Barry Swan set off for the Country Club which lay in its own park some three miles north of Rickenham Green.

The smartly-dressed manager of the Elms Golf and Country Club, to give it its full title, was obliging to the point of obsequiousness; under no circumstances did he want to get on the wrong side of these particular visitors. As far as he knew no patrol cars ventured out to check up on after-hours drinking and that's the way he wanted it to stay. The Country Club was a venue for business lunches, wedding receptions and formal dinners. There was a bar attached to the main function room and another bar used by golfers and members. A few rooms were available for staff but the premises were not residential, a cause of annoyance to the manager as late drinking could then be excused. Catering is not one of the best rewarded careers and he augmented his salary by overcharging on after-hours drinking, generously insisting his staff went home, or to bed if they lived in, and looking after the remaining clients himself. He was too stupid to realize that the irregular hours were known at the police station and it was common knowledge amongst his customers that they were expected to pay a little over the odds for the privilege of a late drink. But there had never been any trouble and the people concerned had the means to pay for taxis home so the status quo was allowed to remain.

The manager, whose name was John Greville, provided them with a duty roster and a list of the guests, the latter a bonus they had not expected but it had been required for the table plans. Ian turned his eyes heavenward as he surveyed it. A hundred and fifty guests for the sit-down meal, the church must have been heaving at the seams. And more had arrived for the dancing in the evening. He asked if there was a telephone he could use, a request which was granted with unctuous alacrity. Greville was beginning to get on his nerves, perhaps he would send a car out cruising one evening, that would knock some of the smarm out of him. Dialling the incident room number he despatched men to the Morleys and the Sutcliffes for the names, addresses and telephone numbers of everyone who was present Saturday night, praying most of them were local.

Meanwhile he and Barry began interviewing members of staff who served at the function, but the next hour or so proved fruitless. It had been far too hectic for any of them to remember anything unusual. The head waiter was summoned from his home half a mile away where he was enjoying his day off. He was the last of the staff to leave and said he ordered two taxis at one thirty but could not remember who they were for. Fortunately Greville was not present to hear these damning words. The bar extension ran out at midnight. This was of no importance to the Chief, his present dilemma was far more significant.

A few minutes before four o'clock the post mortem report landed on his desk. He skimmed through it quickly then settled down to read it in detail. The time of Julia's death was fixed between five and eight a.m. on Sunday, squashing Ian's idea she had died immediately after returning home. The Divisional Surgeon could not be more precise because Mrs Henderson's central heating had remained on. Ian was impressed; narrowing down the time to three hours was a feat in itself after such a long period. Ian thought back. Saturday had not been particularly pleasant, only on Sunday did the sun come out. By Wednesday, when he and Mark were at the football, it was cold again.

The cause of death, he read, was inter-cranial haemorrhage. Stomach contents matched the food on the wedding breakfast menu Ian had taken the precaution of bringing with him from the Country Club, and there were no signs of any toxins other than some alcohol. There were no signs of rape, no recent sexual intercourse and no blood other than the victim's own. All negative aspects. The minute traces of skin under Mrs Henderson's fingernails turned out to be her own, she must have had an itch sometime during the evening.

There was one interesting thing though: tiny pieces of a stonelike material were found in her scalp. They appeared to be earthenware, some bearing traces of sand-coloured paint. Further tests were being made at the moment, but they must be assumed to have come from the murder weapon.

As his men traced and questioned the wedding guests, as the house to house inquiries continued, Detective Chief Inspector Roper went over the report once more. Written there was something so basic, he thought, that he felt it held the clue to the whole thing. If only he could see what it was.

It was another week before he did.

LAURA SUTCLIFFE had been telephoned and was expecting someone to call and, she assumed, under the circumstances, that particular someone would be superior to the young PC who rang her doorbell in the early afternoon to collect a list of the wedding guests.

The news of Julia's death reached her before the telephone call and the arrival of the PC. She learned it through her cleaning lady, Mrs Bedlow, who heard it from a friend. Mrs Bedlow's outraged statement was later confirmed by the local news headlines on the radio. Laura did not switch on the television to see if there were more details to be learned, the set always remained off until six o'clock. It was a rule she adhered to even when the children were small. She somehow feared its influence would be greater than hers and she could not bear that.

Laura was pouring a pre-dinner vodka and tonic when Mrs Bedlow announced the arrival of Detective Sergeant Barry Swan.

'Through here, sir,' she said, straightening her apron and patting her blue rinse affectedly into place.

For once it was not one of her boys bringing the police to the door. 'Dreadful, isn't it?' she began. 'Really dreadful. I always say...'

'Thank you,' Barry interrupted, flashing her what he thought was an irresistible grin, though doubtless Judy Robbins would disagree, and shutting the drawing-room door firmly in her face. She might remain with her ear pressed against it but he was certain she would hear nothing through the thick wood panelling.

Laura offered him a limp hand and asked if he wanted a drink. Unfortunately he had to refuse.

'You obviously knew Mrs Henderson,' he stated. 'Was she a close friend?'

'Not exactly.'

'How do you mean, not exactly, Mrs Sutcliffe?'

'She came here for dinner a few times. To make up the numbers.'

'And when did you last see her?'

'At my son's wedding reception.' Laura's mouth tightened into a thin line showing the creases of dissatisfaction which even her careful make-up could not disguise. Barry saw that despite her sumptuous home and all the evidence of money in abundance, this woman was not happy.

'She was a friend of the Morleys too?' Barry already knew the answer but was curious to hear Mrs Sutcliffe's explanation. Neither family, it seemed, wanted to admit a close connection with Julia. But why?

She hesitated, decided there was no point in lying as the police might already have spoken to Graham who would have taken great pleasure in humiliating her.

'We've been friends of the Morleys for years so naturally we were delighted when Johnny, that's my son, and Helen, their daughter, said they were going to be married. Caroline and I got together one evening and composed the guest list. The usual sort of thing. Family, friends and, naturally, friends of our respective children. Julia Henderson was not on that list.' She paused, looked the detective directly in the eye and said, 'My husband invited her. Unbeknown to either myself or the Morleys.' Her bitterness was unmistakable.

Barry had called in at Northfield Farm before coming to see Mrs Sutcliffe at Longrove Park, a not undeserved name for the palatial house and grounds. The Morleys both expressed their surprise at seeing Julia, and Caroline Morley, trying not to appear the bitch she was, told him she thought it extremely unlikely that Laura was responsible for issuing the invitation. Interesting. Did it mean something had been going on between the deceased and Mr Graham Sutcliffe? If so, Laura Sutcliffe had a not uncommon motive for murder.

'You're sure it was your husband who invited her? Could anyone else have done so?'

'Anyone else? Good heavens, no. I told you, she was not on Caroline's or my list. Unless . . .' Laura bit her lip.

'Unless, Mrs Sutcliffe?'

'Oh, it's nothing.'

'I need to know, madam.' There was a distinct note of warning in Barry's voice. 'You see, we found two invitations in Mrs Henderson's house, and by the thickness of the card it seems unlikely that they were both placed in the same envelope by mistake.'

Laura was shocked. What the man said must be true. She and Caroline painstakingly addressed all the envelopes together, by hand. The invitation card only just fitted. 'So if you have any idea who. . .'

'My son,' she said quietly, turning away in embarrassment. 'My son may have done so.'

'Your son?'

'Yes. Johnny liked her. He mentioned he would like her to be at his wedding but I didn't think he would ask her. She'd been quite decent about the matter of an accident a couple of months ago. Johnny dented her bumper, nothing serious, and she said she wasn't going to bother to report it to her insurers and to forget all about it. Johnny was eternally grateful.' Laura was gabbling, trying to forget the snide remark Graham made to her at the Country Club. What a time to pick, at their son's wedding. 'Anyway, I'm sure he would have told me if he'd done so.' But would he? Laura no longer knew or cared. Life, all of a sudden, seemed unfair.

When Julia first moved to Rickenham Green Laura and Graham took her under their wing. Through Susan Barfoot they learned of the death of her first husband and her separation from her second and Laura, being Laura, assumed the fault lay with Bart whom she had never met and whose name was never mentioned by Julia. They invited her to dinner and introduced her to people she might otherwise not have met. For these actions Julia was grateful. Both Laura and Graham found her to be witty and entertaining and the two women got on as well as Laura's cool reserve would allow. But it was only a short time before Laura noticed the effect Julia had on men. All men. Including her husband. It was then that she dropped her. No explanation was given and Julia accepted this change of affairs with her usual equanimity and humour. Laura's decision was motivated purely by jealousy. All the money she had at her disposal to spend on clothes and beauticians would never provide her with the natural, sexual beauty that was Julia's since adolescence. Laura's own reputation in the town as 'a looker,' which she was in a pale, elegant way, had been usurped and eventually the mention of Julia's name was enough to produce a scornful and derisive flood of words by which no one was deceived. Laura was not sorry she was dead.

Apart from her unfounded fears, the row she had with Graham on the Sunday before the wedding when she discovered he had sent her an invitation more or less confirmed her suspicion that the two were having an affair. Graham had stormed out of the house, not returning until several hours later and offering no explanation as to where he had been. Then, the following Saturday at the reception, she caught him in a corner chatting to Julia, his hand resting on her arm. Only then did she take him to one side and accuse him outright.

'You're going to bed with that slut, aren't you?' she said through gritted teeth, quietly, still trying to smile because appearances counted more than anything.

'She is not a slut,' Graham replied evenly, also smiling, playing her at her own game. 'But *you*, darling, are a jealous bitch.' Then casually, over his shoulder as he went to the bar to get another drink he said, 'and if the question of Julia's morality bothers you so much perhaps you should speak to Johnny about it.'

Laura shook from head to foot, her pink lipstick the only colour showing in her face. Her rage was extreme and barely controllable but she managed to walk stiffly out to the Ladies and wait until it was under control and the contents of her cosmetics bag had restored a semblance of normality. That Graham could accuse their son of such a thing to cover up his own guilt was unbelievable.

Not wishing to spoil Johnny's wedding day and knowing it would look odd if they left early, she struggled through the rest of the evening. She was still seething when their taxi dropped them at their front door but by then enough time had elapsed for her to begin to believe there might be some truth in what Graham had hinted at. It would explain some of Johnny's mysterious absences and the mood swings which she put down to pre-wedding nerves. But what really hurt was the humiliation, the idea that her husband and her son had both slept with the same woman. Her only consolation was the hope that Graham had been kicked out in favour of the younger Sutcliffe.

'Well, well,' Barry thought as he listened to Laura, 'very interesting.' He did not believe the story about the car accident for one minute. It had happened, no doubt, but he suspected it was long forgotten by the privileged Johnny Sutcliffe. With more astuteness than was usual Barry calculated that both men in Laura's life might have been enjoying Mrs Henderson's charms, and if the photographs he'd seen of the lady were anything to go by, who could blame them? But, if his calculations were correct, what would the double insult do to a woman like Mrs Sutcliffe?

'I see, you think your son may have sent the other invitation? And presumably he's now on his honeymoon?'

'Yes. They won't be back until Sunday week.'

'Where and when did he and his wife go, Mrs Sutcliffe?'

'To St Lucia. Their flight was late Saturday night. Only the family knew where they were going, they didn't want any fuss. Helen's a quiet girl, you see, and she was worried about the usual post-wedding pranks. They disappeared to change about seven thirty and my brother-in-law was waiting outside to drive them to the airport. By the time they were missed it was too late, they were well on their way and everyone settled down to enjoy the rest of the evening.'

Newly married Helen Sutcliffe also had a motive for murder if she had any inkling as to what might have been going on but she and Johnny had airtight alibis. Barry grimaced at the unintended pun as he reminded himself that the relationship might have been totally innocent. If the time of their flight checked out they would have been over three thousand miles away when Julia was killed.

Barry was not sure how long it took to fly to the Windward Island; his detective's pay allowed him only such dubious pleasures as a week or two in Spain with whichever girl he was currently seeing. He ascertained which airline they used and made a note to contact them. The fact that two people could definitely be eliminated from the list of possible suspects was the most positive piece of information he'd come up with so far.

He stayed only a few minutes longer, long enough to confirm that, as far as Mrs Sutcliffe was concerned, Julia appeared well and cheerful when she last saw her and that nothing out of the ordinary had occurred at the reception. Barry started to take his leave but stopped at the door to ask one more question.

'How long before you left did Mrs Henderson go?'

'She didn't. That is to say Graham and I were virtually the last to leave but so was Julia. There were several of us waiting for taxis. Two came together and Julia shared with George and Eileen Hart and Susan Barfoot. Graham and I got in the second one. We all drove off at the same time and that was the last time I saw her.' Laura was honest enough to add 'I know she wasn't that well liked but I can't think why anyone would want to kill her. I can only imagine she disturbed a burglar or something. I mean, people don't go around murdering people just because they don't like them, do they.' Barry took this to be a rhetorical question, he could hardly say that, yes, Mrs Sutcliffe, you find out in the police force that sometimes they do.

'Well, thank you very much for your help. What time do you expect your husband?'

Laura looked at her watch. So they had not yet spoken to Graham, but it was, she supposed, better in the long run to be honest.

'You can probably find him in the Crown. It's one of his London days and he usually calls in there on his way back from the station.'

Barry thanked her again and left. He did not blame Graham Sutcliffe for his procrastination. Attractive as she was, his wife did not give the impression she was the sort of woman anyone would want to rush home to.

Barry reversed his car, cruised sedately down the drive and turned out into the lane which led to the High Street. He parked with two wheels on the grass verge of The Green, the only reminder of how the town came by its name. Once, a few cottages surrounded it, which were now much coveted by the wealthy and sold for over-inflated prices. Barry, a town boy through and through, thought it would be more sensible to tarmac over The Green and use it as parking space. He was unable to understand the anger of the conservationists when this was once discussed at a council meeting. He failed to see that just because the town had once been a village consisting of these cottages and the scrubby bit of grass in the middle of them, it was any reason to preserve it. Of course, he couldn't remember it as it once was, a small market town where everyone knew everyone else. It had expanded rapidly, sprawling out to the suburbs over seven square miles of what was once countryside. New roads were built to accommodate the heavy vehicles coming to the trading estates on the outskirts and the High Street, although still the hub of the town, was no longer the main shopping area. This was housed in a precinct with the usual assortment of chain stores and its own multi-storey car-park. Redlands, the large, institutional-looking hospital, was too small to cope with the population. For major surgery for serious accidents, people were taken to Ipswich.

However, a huge, modern, glass structure on the northern side was being erected and was almost complete. This was to become Rickenham General Hospital and was hopefully being opened in July. Rickenham Green, for all its countryfied-sounding name, was as large as, and bigger than, some cities. It now possessed its fair share of high-rise office blocks. With the increase in size and population came additional crime. The town was no longer policed by a handful of men but had its own fully manned, fully equipped police station which served as headquarters for the smaller towns around.

Barry locked the car and walked towards the door of the Crown. This, too, was a listed building and retained all its original character. No false beams and brewery horse brasses here. Barry rarely used the place, typically preferring the more modern pubs where the younger element drank. He pushed open the door, knowing he would be able to recognize Graham Sutcliffe if he was indeed there. Scattered around Laura's very high class drawing-room were numerous family photographs, proudly displayed in silver frames. Her husband was unquestionably the tall, distinguished-looking man with silvery-grey hair, pictured frequently at her side. Either way a pint would not go amiss. But Sutcliffe was there. Barry spotted him immediately.

WHEN THE CHIEF LEFT the incident room and returned to his office, he heard his outside line ringing and hurried in to answer it. It was Moira.

'I'm sorry about last night. It's no excuse, I know, but I was upset at seeing Mark unhappy.'

Ah, last night. How could he have forgotten? Yet it now seemed like a lifetime ago.

'Yes, well, I'm sorry too. You know how I get, the adrenalin was flowing and I hadn't had a chance to wind down properly, even after, well, you know.' Moira did know. 'I didn't mean to be rude.' The apology, if it could be called one, was not so difficult after all. A picture of Brian Lord flashed through his mind and he wondered if, during the lecture, he'd been under some sort of hypnosis as his words often came back to him clearly. Ian took a deep breath and made a conscious effort not to hurry Moira off the line. A minute or two of his time was all she asked and those minutes would not make much difference to the investigations which seemed to be heading nowhere.

'It's all right,' she was saying, 'I didn't realize you were under pressure. I expect you'll be very late?' There was no nagging tone, no reproach in her voice, she was merely stating the obvious.

'More than likely. We're getting the "crazies" already.' They made life so complicated, these people, telephoning, writing and even coming into the station to admit to the crime or to say they knew who had done it, but they all had to be taken seriously. They would look such fools if one of them was telling the truth.

One such man had already called twice in the space of a few hours. He was an exception. His calls were logged but not investigated. He was well known at the station for his confessions. Four or five years ago the Chief did make a fool of himself and wasted valuable time when he sent three squad cars racing over to the council house in Alde Road, from where the call originated, expecting to apprehend a rapist armed with a knife. The only occupant of the terraced house was a registered disabled man, confined to a wheelchair, currently undergoing psychiatric treatment. His treatment was still being continued, as were his confessions, but none of the shrinks had yet come up with a diagnosis. Ian suspected he was simply lonely. The rapist, fortunately, was caught in a neighbouring town several hours later.

'Sorry, Moira, what was I saying? Oh, yes, don't expect me before midnight. Don't wait up. Unless, of course,' and there was teasing laughter in his voice, 'you're studying.' Moira laughed too. It was Ian's subtle way of saying it was all right, he didn't really mind. 'OK. 'Bye. Love you.'

Ian was taken aback. It was some time since she'd said that over the telephone. He glanced around his office, for a moment wondering why he'd returned there. Anyway, at least for the moment, things were back to normal at Belmont Terrace. One less problem to keep him awake tonight.

Unable to recall the purpose of entering his own office he returned to the incident room where he went through statements and jotted down a précis of events so far. It was almost twenty-four hours since the discovery of the body and they were no further forward.

As promised, Bart Henderson had presented himself at Police HQ in Saxborough with an alibi which checked out. Friends in Market Claydon confirmed he was their guest for the weekend and the landlord of the pub where they'd spent all of Saturday evening remembered them well probably, Ian thought, if Henderson's drinking habits were as he believed them to be, because of the added income.

But there were a few hours of the Sunday morning unaccounted for, when Henderson's friends had taken their dog for a long walk, leaving him alone. And a longer period when they were all in bed. Could Henderson have got up in the night, driven across to Rickenham and killed his wife, then returned and pretended to be asleep when they brought him a cup of coffee in the morning? And had he returned again, using those hours when his friends were dog walking, to remove any evidence he might have left behind? Not as impossible as it might at first sound. Someone with Henderson's capacity for alcohol might be capable of driving without mishap, might have persuaded his friends to drink as much as himself to ensure they would not wake in the night, might just conceivably have planned the whole thing in cold blood. The Pearsons, whose hospitality he was enjoying, said he refused point blank to go on the walk with them, saying he hated walking for its own sake. Ian could understand that but surely politeness would demand he acquiesced. But given the amount of alcohol Bart Henderson was rumoured to consume he would not be able to keep up the show for long. If he was guilty they would break him down.

And, as if alcohol was the key word, Barry chose that moment to arrive, smelling distinctly of beer and and cigarette smoke. 'How's it going?' he asked. Ian shook his head. 'Not good. How about you?'

'I think I've trodden on an ants nest at the Sutcliffe place.' Now this was better news. Ian sat down to listen.

'There's a lot going on there under the surface,' Barry continued. 'The wife's a cold bitch. More or less admitted she couldn't stand the sight of Mrs Henderson, and although again she didn't come out with it in so many words, she intimated that her husband was knocking off the deceased. And I got the impression she thought her son might have been too.'

Ian sighed. Intimations. Impressions. Suppositions. All almost as bad as assumptions.

'And?'

'And I spoke to the husband. Pleasant sort of man. I found him in the pub.'

'Yes,' Ian acknowledged. The word spoke volumes.

'Without any prompting Sutcliffe admitted he did have a thing going with Mrs Henderson but it ended some months ago. He described it as an "arrangement". When I asked him exactly what he meant by that he told me they were very fond of each other, mutual comfort, that type of thing, but there was no more to it than that. In other words, nothing serious. My own feelings on it . . .' here Ian not only sighed, he groaned. Now he was to be subjected to Barry's feelings too. The Detective Sergeant took the hint.

'He looked as if he would have liked there to be more. He was not far from tears when he talked about her. Yes, and he also volunteered the information he keeps a flat in London and stays there occasionally when his business demands it. Or that's what he tells his wife. He said his business interests actually take care of themselves nowadays and he uses it to get a bit of breathing space. I suppose he thought we were going to investigate him thoroughly because of his relationship with Mrs Henderson so he might as well come clean about everything. He was not there on the night of the murder, though, he only uses it during the week. When he first mentioned the flat he said "You met my wife" as if that was explanation enough, and I can see what he means. Doesn't rule him out, though. Just because he's been honest so far, everything he told me we would have found out soon enough. And,' here Barry paused for effect, 'he knew about the son.'

Ian's interest was reawakened. If Sutcliffe senior loved Mrs Henderson his jealousy could be a motive all right.

'How did he know? I mean, it's hardly the sort of confession a man about to be married makes to his father, especially if he had any idea of that father's partiality.'

'I don't know as yet whether young Sutcliffe knew about Daddy's philanderings but Graham Sutcliffe became aware of his son's involvement, or what he believes to be an involvement, on the afternoon he told his wife he'd sent Julia Henderson an invitation to the wedding. This piece of news caused a full-scale row and Sutcliffe stormed off. He felt a great desire to see Mrs Henderson, just to talk to, but when he pulled into the lay-by behind her house where he used to leave the car, Johnny's car was already parked there. In itself this meant damn all, but he walked round to the front and the bedroom curtains were pulled across. It was daylight, you see, and there were no net curtains. You know how those new housing estates are, everyone can see into each other's windows. Anyway, Sutcliffe got back into his car and waited. He wanted to be sure it was his son in there. About an hour later

Johnny appeared, he saw him coming out of the back door through the bushes that separate the lay-by from the back garden of 2 Churchill Way. Sutcliffe senior is satisfied and drives off. He told me he didn't blame him, no one could help falling for Julia, and it was probably a last fling before the wedding. So it seems father and son nibbled the same bait,' Barry concluded, lighting up another cigarette.

Not for the first time did Ian wish his partner could be a bit more circumspect in his phraseology.

'In that case,' Ian pointed out, 'it could be any one of the three of them. The Sutcliffes, that is.'

'No. We can rule out young Johnny and his wife. I've already checked with the airline. They boarded and took off for St Lucia on Saturday night as scheduled.'

'Narrows down the field tremendously, doesn't it,' Ian commented caustically, thus deflating Barry's optimistic mood.

'We still have to confirm the second invitation did come from the son and was not sent by some unknown person with the sole purpose of making sure she was there for whatever nefarious reasons. I've got the name of the hotel where they're staying. I might as well do it now.'

'Ruin a man's honeymoon, would you?' Ian joked, in order to make up for his earlier gruffness.

'I'm not sure it will,' Barry said thoughtfully. 'From what Graham Sutcliffe told me, Helen comes from the same mould as Johnny's mother.'

'I thought,' Ian said, 'the saying was that girls married men like their fathers, not the other way around.'

Barry ignored the Chief's joviality and got up to place his call. 'Oh, by the way, what time is it in St Lucia?'

Ian raised his eyebrows. 'How the hell should I know.' That was better, Barry could cope with the boss when he wasn't being playful.

In a short conversation it was confirmed that Johnny had sent the second invitation, or rather, delivered it by hand one evening. Because of the ease with which the conversation was conducted Barry guessed Helen was safely out of earshot. Johnny could be of no further help, there was no one he could think of who could want Julia dead, except maybe his mother, but he kept that thought to himself. He did not sound distraught or ravaged with grief, but it was difficult to judge on the crackling, erratic line.

'By the way,' Barry said, when he'd relayed the conversation to Ian, 'you didn't mention that Mrs Henderson shared a taxi home on Saturday with some people called,' he stopped to look at his notes, 'Hart. A Mr and Mrs Hart, and Susan Barfoot. That narrows it down a bit, they, and the driver, were the last people to see her alive.'

'I didn't mention it because I didn't know,' Ian admitted, wondering why the lovely Mrs Barfoot had not mentioned it. 'A certain lady has been holding back information methinks. Another visit is called for, wouldn't you say? But first we'll have a word with the taxi driver.'

'I'll get on to it right away, sir.' Ian was beginning to think Barry had been taking grovelling lessons from Greville of the Country Club.

It did not take long for Barry to discover which cab company the Club used and a call was put through to them.

'Yes,' the firm's controller agreed when he checked his records, 'they used us a couple of times that evening. One car went out at ten, another at eleven fifteen and two at one thirty. Do you want the drivers' names?' Barry did. 'Here, the controller continued, 'this isn't nothing to do with that murder is it? I don't know what the world's coming to, everyone so violent. Still, I suppose you would know more than most. Let me just check who was on that night.' The controller promised to contact the two drivers and ask them to call in at the station.

'Thank you for your help, it's much appreciated,' Barry told him. 'Marshall' he said to himself as he glanced at the two names he'd written down. It meant nothing. But Bedlow? Where had he heard that before? In two contexts, he believed. There was the Bedlow family who lived on the sprawling council estate, of which two of the boys were always in trouble and a Mrs Bedlow who worked for the Sutcliffes. In a town this size they were probably related.

There was another coincidence too. Mrs Bedlow was a guest at the wedding, this same lady worked for someone who was not sorry to see Julia Henderson dead and someone called Bedlow had been one of the last people to see Mrs Henderson alive. This was looking more like it. Unless it turned out that it was the driver named Marshall who ferried them home.

Andy Bedlow duly arrived at the station and verified he was the son of the same Mrs Bedlow, but, despite Barry's hopes, Julia was not his fare. Mr

Marshall, a man in his early sixties, remembered the
evening clearly as he only worked on Friday and Saturday nights. He had taken the part-time job just over
a year ago to enable him to put a bit more money by
for the time when he was no longer employed full
time. He knew Mrs Henderson, he said, if she ever
needed a taxi she always used their firm. In his opinion she was a lovely woman, polite and friendly and
she always tipped well. He was shocked to learn what
happened to her. Fortunately for Mr Marshall she was
not the last to leave his cab.

'I dropped a couple off at one of the cottages on
The Green,' he recalled, 'never seen them before,
mind, then I went on down the High Street to Churchill Way and Mrs Henderson got out. I waited 'til
she'd got the door open and the lights were on, I always do that for the ladies if they're on their own,
you've got to be so careful these days. Then I took the
Reverend's wife up to the vicarage.' Which was odd,
Barry reflected, as, logically, the vicarage should have
been the first port of call.

'Was there any particular reason you didn't drop
Mrs Barfoot first? Wouldn't that have been quicker?'

'Yes, it would've, but she'd got a man at home and,
like myself, she wanted to make sure her friend got
home safe.'

'Can you remember what they talked about?' Mr
Marshall looked suitably shocked.

'I never eavesdrop on my customers, I listen to my
radio. Besides, I've got to concentrate on the traffic.'
Barry believed him but suspected if he had overheard
anything his loyalty to his customers would prevent

him saying so. Mr Marshall was thanked and shown out.

'I can't understand it,' Ian said. 'She went home alone, the house was in darkness so unless someone was hiding in there no one was waiting for her, and she wasn't killed until much later. Surely she didn't let someone in in the middle of the night. Don't forget, there was no breaking and entering.'

'Unless,' Barry said thoughtfully, 'she left the back door open—people still do, you know—especially if she was expecting a visitor. A lover, maybe, someone she couldn't be seen in public with, another married man.'

'Yes, I see. He let himself in while she was at the reception, Mrs Henderson returns later, they go to bed or talk or whatever and a few hours later quarrel. He kills her and leaves the same way as he came and no one is any the wiser. It seems the only explanation. In which case, who the hell is he?'

'And it still doesn't rule out the wedding guests. It could be someone who left earlier. All their alibis will still have to be checked.'

'I know,' Ian said, feeling bogged down with the possibilities. But he could not lose the gut feeling that whoever killed Julia knew her well, that it was no illicit one night stand who beat her brains to a pulp. He knew—what police officer doesn't?—that most murders are committed by someone close to the victim, but what he felt was pure instinct. There were the few known facts to support his feeling. Apart from no forced entry to the house nothing had been stolen and there had been cash lying around. Nothing seemed to have been disturbed, a stray nutcase would have made more mess. On the other hand there were no signs of sexual activity. The motive, therefore, Ian decided, had to be emotional. The most likely emotion jealousy. And they already knew of several people who harboured such sentiments.

AS SOON AS BARRY LEFT Longrove Park Laura went straight to the telephone. She had to speak to Caroline Morley. Mrs Bedlow, employed for the evening to help with a dinner party, picked up the kitchen extension soundlessly. This was one of the few things at which she was truly adept. She had heard Mr Sutcliffe make his arrangements with the poor, dead woman this way. Mind you, she wouldn't hear a word said against Mrs Henderson, dead or alive, she was a classy one, that one. Nor would she hear anything bad about Mr Graham either come to that. They had both treated her well, spoke to her as an equal, not like that cow Laura who acted like Lady Muck all the time and was no better than she should be. 'Pity she's dead,' she thought as she waited for the telephone to be answered, 'I'd've liked to see them get together permanent.'

'Ah, Caroline. Have the police been to see you yet?' Laura asked.

'Yes, they were here earlier.'

'Before they came to me, I suppose. What did you tell them?'

'Tell them? Only what I knew, dear, that we had absolutely no idea who could have done such a thing, and that it was not either of us who asked Julia to the wedding. There's no need to tell you what my feelings about that woman are as I know you shared my view, but really, the way she used to flaunt herself. One shouldn't, I know, speak ill of the dead but I rather think she asked for it. Innocent people don't get themselves murdered.' Mrs Bedlow suppressed an indignant 'Well I never' and stuffed the tea towel she was holding into the mouthpiece. 'She threw herself at Dennis,' Caroline continued, 'but he was wise to her, he wasn't having any nonsense.' Laura doubted the truthfulness of the statement; she saw the way Dennis undressed Julia with his eyes when his wife's back was turned, just as every other man did.

'Naturally I didn't mention that to the police. You know what they're like, searching for motives everywhere. I wouldn't want them to think I'd done it because she was after Dennis.' Caroline laughed but it was not really a joke, she was having a dig at Laura who, she considered, needed bringing down a peg or two. Just lately she'd been overdoing the Lady of the Manor act. It crossed Caroline's mind that Laura was quite capable of getting rid of the opposition, she was cold enough and she could not be so stupid that she hadn't seen what was going on under her nose. But Caroline was not particularly concerned who it was that was thoughtful enough to remove Julia from the scene; she was simply glad she was no longer around. Recently, although she would never admit it, she was beginning to question Dennis's whereabouts. On one occasion she had gone as far as following him when he went out one evening, which went to show how much influence Julia had over their lives. But Caroline had spent a boring two and a quarter hours huddled in the car outside the Crown. Shielded by the darkness she was able to see through the mullioned window the blurred figure of her husband propping up the bar. He was chatting to Gerry Clayton and only disappeared once, very briefly, presumably to use the Gents. That was fine. Drink she could endure. Another woman, never. Maybe Laura, who she knew mostly slept apart from Graham, felt the same.

'I didn't say anything at the time, Laura, but we were rather taken aback when Julia turned up, especially after some of the things you said about her.'

'Actually, Caroline, it was Johnny who asked her. She was very good over that little matter of the car, if you remember. And we could hardly refuse the boy on his wedding day.'

'So that's your story, is it?' Mrs Bedlow silently remarked. 'Well, the boy may have asked her too but it was me what posted Mr Graham's invitation. He even winked at me when he gave me the money for a stamp.'

'Well, I hope they sort it out quickly, can't say I'm over fond of the police traipsing all over the farm. I suppose they'll speak to all the guests? They asked for a list.'

'Yes,' Laura replied wearily, wishing she had not bothered to telephone, 'I suppose they'll have to. I must go now, we've people coming for dinner. Shall we see you on Sunday as usual?'

'I'll be in touch before then' was the enigmatic reply.

They both hung up and a split second later Mrs Bedlow did the same before returning to the mange tout.

THE LINES TO Rickenham Green police station were not exactly flooded with calls in response to the media appeals for help but two of them concerned Gerry Clayton. Both were anonymous. Both made by women. The first was hissed spitefully down the wires.

'It's Gerry Clayton you want,' the first woman said. 'He's evil. Filthy. A womanizing bastard. You'll see.' The caller sounded more hysterical than logical.

The second caller was more precise, her voice calm and controlled.

'I don't wish to give my name and anyway it'll mean nothing to you as I live in London, but I happen to know the Claytons. May I suggest you inquire into the real reason why Mr Clayton left his last teaching post and moved to your town?' She then gave the name and address of the school where he taught and hung up before the information could be repeated back to her for verification. The grammar, the way in which the message was delivered and the tone of voice suggested the woman had written down what she wanted to say then reeled it off quickly. Perhaps she thought her call could be traced.

'Great,' the Chief said, 'she decides to tell us now, at night. Why not in school time when we could have got on to it right away?' Even as he spoke he was dialling a number. Fifteen minutes later he was satisfied the second call was not a hoax.

He spoke to the officer in charge of the police station nearest to Gerry's old school and found he was in luck. He intended asking for the name and telephone number of the headmaster but it was not necessary. The officer's own daughter was a pupil and the news he imparted was common knowledge locally.

The story was that two fifth formers had made allegations against Gerry Clayton, accusing him of 'interfering' with them. They were loath to be more precise when they made their vague comments to the headmaster and were excused from saying more on account of their tender years. At that point it was only known that 'Sir' sometimes touched them, such gestures as his hand brushing their legs when they leant over his desk. Encouraged by the fifth formers' revelations, a girl in her senior year came forward and said she'd been made love to by Mr Clayton when he gave her a lift home from school one night. She was questioned more fully than the other girls and had to admit, blushing innocently, that no, it couldn't exactly be called rape. It was noted that she had not tried to stop him. Her defence being she was afraid of the consequences if she refused as Mr Clayton was giving her extra tuition for her 'A' levels. It was also noted that no direct threat had been made or even implied. But the damage was done.

The girl was already eighteen, having been kept back a year, and no criminal charges were brought to bear. Gerry had no choice but to resign on the spot. He knew that at the next Parent/Teacher Association meeting his resignation would be demanded, it was only a matter of time. In the eyes of his colleagues it was not the action he was accused of that was so damning but the scandal he'd involved them in. He had made them feel unclean and, of course, at the back of one or two minds was the thought that it could easily have been themselves.

This, then, was the reason for his sudden move in the middle of term-time and why he was quite content to take a dead end job at the Morleys' farm. His excuse that Ann did not want to move until the house was ready was partly true but Ian could see that she, wishing to continue a teaching career, had remained at her job in a different school until the half-term holidays. What any of this had to do with the murder of Julia Henderson he failed to see, but was it purely coincidental that this particularly nasty crime took place not long after Clayton's arrival in the town? It was a straw, the first in all this mess, but it was a straw. Ian put on his coat. He was going to have a quiet word with Mr Gerry Clayton.

'Do you want me to come?' Barry inquired. Ian grunted, it could have meant anything but Barry decided to take it to mean yes.

'Hang on then, I'll just get my mac.'

Ian sat down again to wait. He rubbed his eyes and looked around the room realizing he'd never really taken much notice of his surroundings since their move four years ago. The building the Rickenham Green Division of the police now occupied was new, purpose built in fact and although it was more convenient, better furnished and certainly warmer than the old station, it had none of its character. The green and cream painted corridors of the old building exuded the particular odour of all police stations. Mingled with the smells associated with all decaying buildings were those of canteen food, linoleum polish and cigarette smoke. The mildew-stained corners of the interview rooms spoke of years of frightened sweat and the cloying cheap perfume of prostitutes, but were only the result of wind-driven rain which eventually found its way into the crumbling brick. The new headquarters were clean, bright and antiseptic and would take many years to acquire a personality of their

own. Ian was in favour of the No Smoking areas; he
had given up just before the move. Here, there were no
ancient tobacco tins and saucers making do as recep-
tacles for dog-ends but the heavy, cut-glass ashtrays on
the desks of those who smoked were less homely. Ian
wanted to put back the clock and knew, as he thought
it, it was a sign he was getting older.

Barry returned wearing a beige, baggy raincoat, no
doubt the latest fashion, but in Ian's opinion it looked
as if his companion had not been able to find one his
size. Together they made for the stairs, told the duty
sergeant where they could be found if needed, pushed
through the gleaming chrome and glass swing doors at
the entrance of the building and walked to the car-
park.

NEITHER GERRY NOR ANN slept that night. After
restlessly tossing and turning for several hours they
gave up all pretence of trying and got up. They sat in
their new living-room, a room in which a new life
should be beginning, and shared the last bottle of
Ann's wine. She wondered how Gerry could bear to
drink it under the circumstances but it was all they had
in. Tomorrow she would stock up at the off license; it
was not going to be an easy weekend.

'I thought it was all over,' Gerry said, finally
breaking the silence. 'I really thought if we moved
away and made a completely new start we could put it
all behind us. Oh, Ann, I'm...' he could not continue. He bowed his head and, elbows on knees,
pushed his hands through his hair. Ann got up to refill their glasses, squeezing one of his hands on the
way. She noticed there were no longer any traces of

fingerprinting ink. She could not understand it, his prints matched some of those found in Julia's house yet he denied ever setting foot inside. And she did not think he was lying; he believed he had not crossed her threshold. The only alternative was that he had but could not remember. Perhaps, as one of the parents of the girls who had complained suggested, he was mentally ill. Sick was the word she actually used. Was it possible he did things without knowing? And if so? That idea was pushed firmly away.

She placed the full glass on the side table and leaned over to stroke his longish, grey-streaked hair. She was well aware his pupils found him attractive, had always been aware of the dangers involved in a handsome man standing in front of a class of girls of that age, girls who nowadays, at sixteen and seventeen, were already women. He was not classically good looking, his face being rugged, as if the features and the strong lines surrounding them had been carved, but it was a face that was alive and interesting, and he was in good shape although he did not exercise. He was the sort of man she, in her youth, would have fallen for but she had not met him until she was well into her twenties and regretted the years they had not had together. She loved him but there was nothing she could do for him except stand by him.

'I didn't do it,' Gerry told her, 'I found her attractive, I admit, more than attractive, she was a beautiful woman, but I never touched her, I swear it. I'd learned my lesson, Ann. That one time was the only time.' She said nothing. What could she say? The uncertainty would remain with her always: having been unfaithful once he might be again. But to murder someone? No, it was not possible.

'Well, at least they haven't charged me,' he said, seeing the sadness in her eyes and wishing to make amends. No, she thought, but they have asked us not to leave the town, which means they're thinking about it.

AFTER THE SESSION with Clayton, Ian wondered briefly if, having suffered enough over the schoolgirl business, Ann had been driven to the limits of sanity by her husband's flirting, or more, with Mrs Henderson. The man admitted he was attracted to her. But after talking to Ann he changed his mind. She loved her husband, that was obvious, and seemed prepared to stick by him. She struck him as intelligent, sensible and not the sort of person to fly into a murderous rage. Neither did she appear capable of cold-bloodedly planning and executing a killing. He agreed with Barry, though, there was something about Clayton that did not ring true. He was not exactly lying but he wasn't coming clean either. At least now they had definite proof he had been in the house, despite his denial. Fingerprints did not appear of their own accord. Strange that he should continue to deny it. If they were on friendly terms there was no reason why she should not have invited him in. The man was hiding something and Ian's own rough-handling technique had not been successful in discovering what. He decided to ask Brian Lord to have a word with him. Okay, he did not like the idea of police psychologists but if they had to have one on the payroll, then let him earn that pay.

The inquest was to be held on Monday and would be a formality. The Coroner would pass a verdict of murder by person or persons unknown to enable the body to be released and the funeral arranged. But by whom? Bart Henderson presumably. He was the only one with a vague legal relationship to her although they were no longer married. This new fact had been confirmed when Sergeant Baker spoke to Julia's solicitor during the afternoon. The conversation was deferential on the one side and rather patronizing on the other. Sergeant Baker and the solicitor in question had occasionally expressed differing views in the witness box of the local courthouse. It transpired that Julia Henderson was not in possession of her decree absolute but the papers were ready to be sent to her. The solicitor hoped there would be no problem over the matter of his fees. He ended the conversation by agreeing to have a copy of Mrs Henderson's will available for inspection.

It had been another long day and the Chief went home in time to catch the beginning of a late film which Moira wanted to watch. The screen flickered before him but little of the action or dialogue penetrated his mind. Three names revolved in his head: Gerry Clayton, Bart Henderson and Laura Sutcliffe. A fit woman would have the strength to knock another woman unconscious with a blow from a heavy object; after that it would be easy enough to complete the job. It was illogical to think of Mrs Sutcliffe as the most likely suspect when he had not yet met her, especially as there were probably other suspects as yet undiscovered. Good God, there was still the rest of the guest list to get through. Conceivably something which happened at the reception might have precipitated the woman's death. And there was Susan Barfoot to be re-questioned. She had omitted to tell them about shar-ing a taxi with the deceased, and in their last words together might lie a vital clue.

The names continued to go round and round. Gerry Clayton, known to be lying. Laura Sutcliffe, cold, calculating and jealous and Bart Henderson, whose fingerprints had also been found. There were too many suspects and not one single substantial motive.

FIVE

On Friday the atmosphere at the vicarage could be cut with a knife. Michael knew his wife's moods, sensed her agitation and despair and was powerless to do anything about it. Since first hearing the news of Julia's death she was unable to keep still, flitting from one chore to the next. Michael realized it might take months before she came to terms with the loss of her friend but hoped, meanwhile, she would not wear herself out.

He was not unaffected himself. His nerves were no longer steady and he found it difficult to sleep. Hopefully that would wear off. He knew he was lucky, he was one of the few men who had not given in to Julia's allure. And she had more than her fair share of that. Susan was, and always would be, the only woman he wanted to desire. He watched her pale, tired face as she dusted his study and wished she could rest. His desk already gleamed but he dutifully picked up the papers containing scribbled notes for Sunday's sermon as she approached it.

'Leave it, Susan, you look shattered,' he told her, placing his large hand over hers as she began to rub away at an imaginary mark. 'Sit down, I'll make us some coffee.'

'No. I don't have time. There's a meeting here this afternoon. Or had you forgotten?' It was not like her to be sharp but her tone was masking the emotions she held tenuously at bay. Michael nodded but said nothing. He was disappointed when she did not agree to cancel the meeting, people would have understood, but she insisted they went ahead with it.

Of the two, Michael was far less organized. Left alone he would have drifted through life, helping others wherever he could, not becoming over-anxious if he failed and managing to turn up for church services on time. Since his marriage to Susan his life ran like clockwork. Naturally, with two young boys certain things needed to be done at certain times, regular meals, for instance, and sensible bedtimes. Over the years he became used to her ways and made them his own. The one thing he really envied Susan was her ability to rise early no matter how late she went to bed the night before. He had never been a morning person. Every day, including Sundays, she was up, washed and dressed, hair neatly tied back in a pony tail ready to serve breakfast at the large, wooden table in the kitchen at seven thirty. It was a meal she insisted they ate, although Michael would have made do with several cups of tea, and the only meal they ate in the kitchen. On the mornings Michael was not out on calls or busy elsewhere, he observed her daily routine with amusement. Once the boys left for school she washed the dishes, cleaned the kitchen then polished and vacuumed the downstairs rooms. While the hall floor was drying she did the bedrooms and the bathroom. Michael could not remember a single occasion when his home was not spotlessly clean and he was proud of the way she managed to look after everything so well. 'You provide my home for me,' she once told him, 'it's my job to keep it nice for you.' He often thought a lot of her work was unnecessary, it was not such a major crisis if there were specks of dust on the furniture, but Susan was a perfectionist, perpetual cleaning and polishing was as much a part of her as the necessity of breathing.

She stood at the window, wiping the sill with a damp cloth. There was a paperclip on the floor beside Michael's chair and she bent down gracefully to retrieve it giving him a full view of her narrow waist and her slim hips outlined by the jeans she wore for housework.

'It's the same with everything,' he thought as a wave of sympathy struck him, 'whatever must she go through every day? Always seeking the unattainable, the everlasting fight against dirt, the endless war against gaining weight.' If she gained a few ounces she dieted immediately, but this did not prevent her from making wholesome puddings for him and the boys, and never, of course, out of packets.

Michael's sermon was almost complete, it only needed a few finishing touches before it was ready for Susan to type. He usually gave it a final once-over on Saturday morning when it would be fresher and he could be more objective. He remembered the fire and brimstone bit for Tom Prendergast. The meeting was not due to start until three; he would use the intervening hours to take his wife out somewhere. It need not be far, they could just get in the car and go for a run, anything but this domesticity. She might like to walk in the woods as they used to when they seemed to have more time, the tranquillity might do her good, give her a chance to talk to him and let him take some of the burden of her grief. Or he could take her out to lunch, buy her a dress, anything she wanted, whatever it took to end her silence, to bring her back to him.

'Susan?' She replaced the ornament she was dusting and looked up blankly, as if she did not recognize him. 'Susan, come here a minute.' He stood up and moved towards her, gently taking the duster from her hand. 'I know how you feel but you can't keep it inside you. Let's go out. Just the two of us. Come on, I've finished here. No, no arguments, go and get your coat and we'll go.' At least his words produced a reaction.

'No,' she said, 'I can't. Not like this.' She waved a hand at her jeans. 'I'm too untidy.' Michael kissed her forehead, surprised to find it cold and clammy.

'Of course you can, you look lovely.'

'No. What on earth would people think?'

'It really doesn't matter what people think.'

'Oh, but you're wrong, Michael, it does. It matters very much.'

She turned away and left the room. Michael sat down and waited, assuming she had gone upstairs to change. His heart sank when he heard the chink of crockery coming from the kitchen and, when he went to investigate, saw Susan standing at the work counter measuring flour into a bowl.

He brushed aside his exasperation and asked as calmly as he was able 'What on earth are you doing? I thought we were going out.'

'Baking,' she retorted brusquely. Her back was to him, she did not turn around. 'I can't go out, there's too much to do. You do realize, don't you, that in a few hours there'll be twelve people here expecting tea and sandwiches.'

Michael's patience reached its limits. 'I know exactly how many people will be here, the same as every
month. Including us it makes fourteen, then Matthew
and Josh will be home from school expecting their tea.
Now come on, Susan, there's no need for all this; give
yourself a break. You spoil everyone except yourself
and right now you need a bit of spoiling. Look, you
won't let me cancel the meeting so how about a compromise? When I go over to St Bartholomew's we get
a cup of tea and a plate of good old digestive biscuits,
can't you do the same for once?' Susan's expression
conveyed her opinion on the quality of the teas at St
Bart's. She carried on rubbing the fat into the flour.

'And as for the boys,' Michael reasoned, 'how can
they appreciate your cooking unless they're allowed to
eat junk food now and again? *I'll* do their meal tonight, we'll stop at Stacey's on the way back and get
something from the deep freeze, fish fingers or something, they'll enjoy that for a change. Now, leave that
and come with me.' He firmly pulled the bowl away
and placed it in the fridge, unsure if that was the right
thing to do with it but determined to get her out of the
house. To his surprise she offered no further argument.

He suspected she was prolonging the time until she
would have to face neighbours and parishioners and
hear their various condolences. Tomorrow was Saturday, the day she did the weekend shopping, she
could not avoid seeing many of them in Fine Fare, it
might be easier to get some of them out of the way today when he could be with her.

'No, not in the car,' she said as Michael unlocked
the doors. 'Can we just look around the shops?'

'Yes, if that's what you want.' So his suspicions were correct. He was disappointed he would not have her to himself but he would be a buffer against the painful reminders. Every few yards acquaintances stopped to say a few words, some had heard the news, others would not be aware of it until they listened to the local radio station or read it in the *Rickenham Herald*. Susan bore their words bravely, her elfin face white but with a gentle smile for everyone. No one had a bad word to say against Julia, people who hardly knew her claimed longstanding friendship. Of course, from their point of view it was the most exciting event in Rickenham Green for years and outstripped the wedding as a conversation piece.

The weather was mild again, still undecided if summer was imminent, but a fine drizzle hung in the air. When they returned to the vicarage Susan's hair, which she had released from its elastic band before going out, was fluffed out softly around her face, the dampness giving it body, and there was some colour in her cheeks. By the time the meeting began and she'd taken her place at the large rectory table they had bought cheaply some years ago, she felt the worst was over and was able to put her mind to the matters discussed in her usual efficient way.

'My dear child, under the circumstances...' the rector from St Bartholomew's began, waving away Susan's apology for the lack of homemade tarts and cake, but secretly he was relieved he would not have to report to his wife on the feast normally provided. Only when this break for tea came did she begin to feel the flutterings in the base of her stomach, a sign she knew well. She should not have gone out. She had let Michael down. There had been time to prepare a plate of sandwiches but the biscuits and cake were shop bought. If only she had remained at home and baked as she intended. She excused herself by saying she was going to make more tea and got to the kitchen seconds before the shaking started. Once safely there she stood on the kitchen steps and reached for the small, brown, plastic bottle hidden in the top cupboard. Inside the bottle was the only thing which kept her going, the guarantee of perfection, or perfection the way she envisaged it. Without the Valium she was unable to function. Despite the concern for the indiscriminate use of tranquillizers and sedatives, they were still relatively simple to get hold of if you knew the right person. An old college boyfriend was a doctor in a neighbouring town and it was to him that Susan went for the repeat prescription, and it was in that town, where she was not known, that she got the prescription filled. It would never, ever, do for anyone in Rickenham to become aware that she was anything other than she appeared. She enjoyed the occasional cigarette, too, but not in front of the boys and only ever at home. Michael knew she smoked, of course, she did so freely in front of him, but he did not know about the Valium.

It did not cross her mind that there was a far simpler remedy, that she could ease up a bit. She felt no envy of people who were less hard on themselves, people like Julia, who never seemed to mind leaving dishes in the sink over night if she was too tired or too lazy to wash up, or like Mrs Bedlow, who, whilst more than happy to go out and clean someone else's house with great vigour, lived in conditions which were not actually, but were considered by Susan, filthy. It was they who had the problem, not she.

She returned to the meeting. The large teapot was now replenished and she poured it with a steady hand.

LATER, after their guests departed and Susan was putting away the tea things, Matthew Barfoot and Mark Roper made their way home from school, loitering at the end of the vicarage driveway to make their arrangements for the weekend. Josh was already back; still at primary school, he came out twenty minutes earlier. Matthew was almost silent as they walked, grunting non-committally to his friend's chatter. Although there was a year's difference in their ages they got on well and usually enjoyed each other's company. Mark was not particularly mature for his age but he was a sensible boy, quiet and sometimes introspective, much the same as Matthew. Lately Mark was beginning to wonder if Matthew was outgrowing him. He didn't talk much now and the past day or so he'd made Mark feel a hindrance, as if he was in the way.

They stood together at the gate, Matthew taller by some two inches, both blond, but where Mark's features still held traces of boyhood, Matthew's face was leaner, his jaw, which he already shaved, angled. He was good looking and because of his athletic build, was often taken for several years older. There was something in Matthew's face which drew people to him, an undefinable haunted intelligence.

Mark knew he must be grieving over Julia's death. She was a particular friend to him, a relationship he didn't quite understand himself, but accepted. Maybe that was the problem. He had, too, been complaining of headaches and feeling sick all week, so it could be he was simply going down with something. All Mark hoped was that he was not going to lose him as a friend. There was a little consolation in the thought that now it was May the football season was at an end, at least for the school—it never seemed to end on the television—and a few more of his mates would be available on Saturdays.

He and Matthew never had any definite weekend plans. They would meet and walk around, sometimes aimlessly in the town, or down by the river. A few years ago they spent a lot of time on their bikes, cycling round the lanes or repairing them in the ramshackle garage at the vicarage. Somewhere during the past year they had outgrown this occupation. They both agreed that Rickenham Green was boring, that there was nothing to do, but couldn't actually say what it was they wanted to do. They had some good laughs, though, if they met up with a crowd in the town centre. Occasionally they'd share one of the cigarettes Matthew took from a packet his mother thought was well hidden. She must be daft to think he didn't know she smoked. Other times, pocket money permitting, they bought a McDonalds to eat on the way home. Despite Moira's remonstrations it never spoiled Mark's appetite for lunch. Susan remained unaware that her son ate anything beyond school dinners and the well-balanced meals prepared by her own hands.

Matthew was not the only one who was fed up that Friday. Mark told him he'd formed the opinion his father didn't seem to like him. He knew he'd only been taken to football on Wednesday because he'd heard his mother shouting the odds about it. 'He's always got things on his mind. If you talk to him he doesn't hear you. I don't know why I bloody well bother.'

'You think you've got problems. You've got no idea, you idiot.' Mark was surprised at the venom in his voice. 'Your Dad's a sodding saint compared to my mother. All the time she pretends she's so wonderful, all those boring things she does for the church. I hate it. I don't go any more and they can't make me. And now I can't even talk to Julia any more.' Matthew turned his head away. Mark realized he was crying and knew he must be embarrassed. Good friends though they were it was not the sort of thing they exposed to one another. 'See you,' he said, and hurried down the vicarage drive. Mark was left none the wiser. If he wanted to be like that and not confide in him, he'd find someone else to knock around with tomorrow. He knew how much Julia meant to him and wondered, as he strolled home, whether he was upset because he would have preferred it to have been his mother who was killed. Her death had shaken him up, too, although he didn't know her as well. With Matthew it was always Julia this and Julia that. He forgot his own reaction when he listened to the news yesterday evening. He'd got in from school and done an hour's homework then wandered downstairs to get a bowl of cereal to tide him over until his meal was ready. He took it into the front room to join his mother who was listening to the news. His hopes of spending any time with his father over the weekend were dashed as he listened to the local news headlines and suddenly understood what the local newsreader was saying. Julia Henderson was dead. Killed in her own home. He knew Julia, had seen her at Matthew's house a few times and even been to her house himself with Matthew, but at that moment he hated her. Hated her because she would be taking his father away from him again, at least until he found her killer. Then, no doubt, there'd be something else.

To Moira's astonishment he banged the bowl on the coffee table, said 'Oh shit' quite audibly and stumped upstairs to his room. She heard his bedroom door slam shut behind him. It was after this episode she rang Ian at the station to satisfy herself there was no longer any bad feeling between them, that at least one of the males in her life was temporarily all right. Mark had come down later, his mood slightly improved, and they ate their meal together. There was no point in waiting for Ian, he was into the second day of his inquiries and had no idea what time he'd be home. As Mark tucked into his food and they talked, his ready smile was soon back on his face.

When Mark entered the house on that Friday night he seemed puzzled. Moira ruffled his hair, she knew better than to try to kiss him. 'What's up?'

'I don't know. It's Matthew.'

'Have you had a quarrel?'

'Not exactly, but he's been funny all week. Probably because of Julia.'

'Julia?' Did he mean the dead woman?

'Yea, he used to go and see her quite a bit.' That would explain it. Moira knew the Barfoots only slightly, she and Ian were not churchgoers, and from what she had heard Susan was the perfect vicar's wife but secretly she wondered if she gave any time to her sons. If she was right it was natural Matthew would look elsewhere for attention. When he came to the house he was always polite and respectful as he'd been brought up to be, but she felt there was something wrong. He seemed old for his years, self-sufficient and not suffering all the anguish of a fifteen year old. Yet underneath it she sensed he might be lonely.

Mark brightened up considerably when the phone rang just after eight. It was Matthew. He said nothing about what had happened earlier, just that he'd meet him in the morning if he liked. This time a definite arrangement was agreed and Mark went upstairs to finish off his homework.

SATURDAY MORNING DAWNED cloudy and grey. The air was heavy but Ian's spirits were lifted. He felt he might be getting somewhere. Friday was a wash-out as far as the investigation went. No further clues, no leads, but the door-to-door inquiries were complete and anyone who knew Julia Henderson had been seen. The day had been spent in checking and cross-referencing statements. Already there were one or two discrepancies and several of the people interviewed were becoming rattled. That was the time to strike. Lost tempers gave many a criminal away. Overnight, as he slept, Ian's priorities had become miraculously sorted out. First thing, he intended to see Mrs Barfoot, that done he would travel up to Saxborough to interview Bart Henderson. Harry Watkins told him he would be only too pleased to have him on his patch; if there was time for a pint they could go over old times. Barry was to continue with the wedding guests, if anything looked useful he was to pass the telephoning on to someone else and pay a personal visit, distance allowing of course. Then, and this would be interesting, Barry was to have the Sutcliffes brought down to the station and question them together. This was a deliberate ploy, Ian knew what being hauled in for questioning would do to people like them. And they would undoubtedly behave differently in the interrogation room from the way they did in their magnificent home.

Ian poked his head into the incident room and, satisfied his instructions were understood and that nothing new had come in during the night, went to the vicarage.

Susan opened the door, smiled her wan smile and invited him in. Today she wore a pretty floral skirt and a plain white blouse and her hair hung loosely around her shoulders. She explained she had just returned from the supermarket and was in the middle of unpacking the groceries.

'I'll put the kettle on. You don't mind the kitchen?' Ian said he didn't and followed her down the hallway, his stomach rumbling appreciatively as the warm aroma of baking filled his nostrils. On cooling trays lay a batch of scones and a pie he guessed to be apple. To atone for her laziness of yesterday Susan got up earlier than usual and made them before she went out. Moira, Ian knew, was a very good housewife but Mrs Barfoot would take all the prizes. He'd noticed, as she showed him in, that the two main rooms off the hall were immaculate, as was the kitchen in which he now stood. All this had been accomplished and the shopping done and it was only just after ten. Susan reached and stooped, carefully arranging groceries and vegetables in their appropriate places while she waited for the kettle to boil.

'You didn't mention it yesterday, I'm sure it was the last thing on your mind,' Ian began with caution, not wishing to cause her further distress, 'but I believe you and Mrs Henderson shared a taxi home last Saturday night, from the Country Club.'

Susan's face was hidden by the open door of the fridge.

'Yes,' she replied, with no more than a second's hesitation, 'we did. I'm sorry, I forgot all about it. Is it important?'

'The fact in itself isn't, we know the taxi dropped your friend off first, then brought you back here. But I am interested in any conversation which may have taken place between you. Can you recall what you talked about? Was there anything she said which might be relevant to what happened? Was she expecting a visitor for instance?'

Susan stood up, the unpacking finished, and spooned coffee into two mugs then filled them with boiling water.

'Instant I'm afraid.' Her face was drained of colour. She handed him a mug and placed a jug of milk and a bowl of brown sugar on the table.

'I'm sorry to bring it up again, Mrs Barfoot, but the fact is, apart from her killer, you and the taxi driver were the last people to see her alive.'

'I'm sorry, Chief Inspector, but I can't tell you very much that'll be of help. We talked mainly about the wedding; you know, gossip. What people wore, who was dancing with whom, that sort of thing. Can't the driver remember?'

Ian ignored the question. He noticed Susan's dainty hands were clasped around her mug as if she was cold.

Her short nails were even and white-tipped, natural
and healthy looking. He took in her silky, clean hair
and spotless clothes and thought she must take as
much care of herself as she did of her home.

'Mum?' A blond head, apparently belonging to a
boy of about ten, appeared around the door. 'Can I go
over to Dean's house?'

Susan checked the time on the cooker clock. 'Yes.
As long as you're back by half past twelve. Have you
got your watch on?' Punctuality was one of the things
she instilled into the boys.

'Yes. Thanks, see you later.' Then with a quick grin
at the visitor he was gone. They had recognized each
other from Ian's first visit.

'That was Josh, my youngest. Matthew's out
with...' Her hand flew to her mouth, not quite con-
cealing a very attractive smile. 'Oh, I've just realized,
you're Mark's father, of course.'

'Yes, I am,' Ian said, bewildered. How on earth did
she know?

'They're in the same class, they're always off together, doing whatever it is boys of that age do. Well,
you know that of course.'

But Ian did not know. He flushed slightly, ashamed
that he had not taken in the names of his son's friends,
and hoped his embarrassment did not show.

'Ah, yes, Matthew. Well, if there's nothing else you
can think of, Mrs Barfoot, I'll be on my way. But if
you do recall anything Mrs Henderson said that might
help us, please let me know.'

With one last, longing look at the cooling trays, Ian
allowed himself to be shown out. Something had attracted his attention whilst he sat at the kitchen table,

but whatever it was went out of his mind when Mark's name was mentioned. Now, as he stepped aside to let Susan open the front door, over the smell of baking he caught the faintest whiff of a not unpleasant smell he felt he should be familiar with. For the moment he couldn't place it. By the time he returned to the station he had forgotten all about it.

BARRY HAD LITTLE SUCCESS with his boring job of ringing round the remainder of the guests. Very few of the people from out of town knew who Julia was and even with the description he gave only one or two even remembered seeing her. Personally he thought the whole exercise was a waste of time when he could be concentrating on finding enough proof to arrest Gerry Clayton. He hoped the Chief would not forget whose instinct it was that led them to the guilty party when the credits were being handed out.

'There's not enough evidence. Not any really. I know he lied but that does not make him a murderer,' Ian remonstrated when Barry voiced his complaint. 'In an inquiry of this sort you have to remain totally objective if you're to get anywhere.' There was no suitable answer to this but Barry was sure Clayton wasn't going anywhere, his wife would see to that, and they had both given their assurance on this point. If, and when, new evidence came to light he would take great pleasure in gloating. For now the search must continue.

Ian decided to risk one pint of Adnams before setting off for Saxborough. His head ached with anxiety and lack of sleep but that did not put him off his beer. He decided some fresh air might do him good and walked down as far as the Crown. Henderson had been told to expect him sometime during the afternoon so there was no desperate hurry. He would treat himself to a jumbo sausage with fried onions in French bread and prayed Moira didn't hear of it. It was in the pub he struck lucky.

'Pint?' the landlord inquired. Ian nodded and before his conscience got the better of him, placed his order for lunch. He carried his drink across to a small table in a corner by the window and sipped it slowly. He was in the mood to down half of it in one go, but dared not. There would not be enough left to wash down his food and he could not risk a second pint with a drive in front of him, and there was no way the Detective Chief Inspector was going to be seen sitting in a pub nursing a soft drink. He sat back, relaxing slightly as his eyes wandered over the other occupants of the bar. There were one or two couples enjoying a drink after their shopping, the evidence of this showing in the full carrier bags scattered between the table legs. Propped against the bar was one of the Bedlow boys, a pint of lager at his elbow. He looked across at Ian, acknowledged his presence with a nod of his head then looked away again. And also at the bar stood Tom Prendergast in the process of paying for refill. When he turned round to return to his seat Ian smiled and beckoned him over. He'd known him for years, a nice old man under the façade of grumpiness.

'Hi, Tom, have a seat. How's it going?'

'Can't complain. You?'

'Well, at the moment...'

'It's all right, you don't need to tell me, it shows on your face. Must be a real headache, this 'ere murder.

I liked the Henderson woman, you know. She was one of the good 'uns.'

Ever since he moved to his cottage on The Green, Tom and Julia had been on speaking terms. Tom's son and daughter-in-law now ran the farm he'd worked all his life and at first he could not be persuaded to move to the cottage that had been in the family for years. When the previous occupant, Tom's cousin, died, the place remained empty although several estate agents in the town tried to get their hands on it. Eventually Tom's son talked him into the move, using as his argument the possible decay of the building if it was not inhabited soon. It was not a case of wanting him out of the way, his family were more than fond of him, but Tom was nearing eighty and as long as he remained at the farm, refused to take it easy. A compromise was struck whereby his daughter-in-law came in twice a week to clean for him and leave him a hot meal. In return he walked up on Wednesdays and gave a hand with whatever needed doing. He also spent the weekends at the farm. It was during the second week after he moved, while he was still readjusting, that he met Julia. He was sitting on the bench that circled one of the few remaining trees on The Green when he spotted her strolling along enjoying the sunshine. As she neared he raised his hat, chuckling to himself at the wicked thought that not many years ago it would have been more than his hat that was raised at the sight of such a beautiful woman. She stopped to pass the time of day and their friendship started from that point. She was never too busy to have a word with him if they happened to meet and she always remembered to ask how his arthritis was. Tom thought she was a lovely woman and said as much to Ian again.

'Can't think who'd want to go and do a thing like that, I can't get over it. S'pose you've questioned her husband?'

'Yes.' Ian could admit that much. He did not want old Tom to think he wasn't doing his job, but that was as far as he could go.

'He went to see her the other week, he did. On a Sunday it was. I know because I saw him as I was on my way to the Coach and Horses down her end of the town. Great big parcel he was taking to her. Some sort of lamp she told me it was when I saw her later in the week. Can't imagine what she'd want a great thing like that for. Myself now, I like a good, strong ceiling light.'

Ian was only half listening but suddenly his attention was fully captured. Life was strange. All the questions they'd asked, all the people interviewed, and what did they come up with? A great big nothing. And now, because he had a headache and decided to walk to the Crown instead of going to the Feathers, which was nearer, this gem had been delivered in the course of a friendly conversation. So Bart Henderson had recently visited his wife. Ex-wife. Dead wife. Interesting.

'When did you say this was, Tom?' Ian asked as casually as he could.

'Now, let me see it wasn't last weekend because Brenda came down for me early. She usually picks me up at the Coach and Horses about one, after I've had a couple of pints. Makes the Sunday dinner all the better, a couple of pints first. No, last week she was

doing one of those barbecue things, she picked the
right day too, it was lovely and warm. We were all
there, both my sons and their wives and the grandchildren. Not the same as a roast though, is it?' Ian
concealed his impatience. He knew Tom of old and if
he gave the slightest indication that what he was saying was of any importance the man was quite capable
of embellishing history with 'facts' from his vivid
imagination. There was a pause as Tom stuffed some
dark, nasty-looking shreds into his pipe then lit it, using the old ploy to gain time, to give his failing memory a chance.

He took the pipe from his mouth and held it in front
of him, contemplating it as if it had only that moment come into his possession. At last he spoke.

'It weren't the Sunday before that either because my
arthritis was playing up bad, the weather, you know,
the rain don't half make a difference. I stayed up at the
farm that Saturday night, slept in my old bed, too. It
wasn't the same without May, nothing's been the same
since she went.' Ian made sympathetic noises, knowing how hard Tom's wife's death had hit him. 'So it
must have been the week before that. Yes, I'm sure
I'm right, three weeks ago. Time goes on so quick
these days, seems like yesterday.'

So Bart had visited Julia within the last three to six
weeks. Ian had to give Tom that much leeway. He had
noticed the lighting-up strategy, he'd used the same
technique himself in the days when he smoked. But the
sixty-four dollar question was was it Bart's last visit?

'Well, I'm pleased for her sake she and her husband remained on friendly terms after they parted,'
Ian commented hoping that Tom had been in Julia's

confidence and that he would take the bait and offer some more information.

'Oh, Julia'd get on with anyone, she would. She said her old man was all right, a good sort, but not the right man for her. She married him on the rebound, I reckon, after the first one went and got himself killed.' Ian already knew about Brian Davis. Copies of his birth and death certificates, along with a copy of the marriage certificate of himself and Julia, were found in a buff file on their own in the bottom of Julia's bureau. Susan Barfoot, in her initial conversation with the Chief Inspector, had spoken of him and she, like Tom, was of the opinion that Julia never really recovered from his death. He was killed in a motorway pileup one foggy night, through no fault of his own. A lorry, travelling too fast for the conditions, ploughed into the back of his car before swerving across all three lanes, killing not only Brian Davis but three other people as well. Julia was left widowed and childless and the Chief could only hope there had been some small consolation in the knowledge she was not left penniless also. Naturally, in the light of what had happened to Julia, the circumstances of her first husband's death were checked but there were no clues there, it was a run-of-the-mill road traffic accident.

'I think . . . what was his name?'

'Mrs Henderson's husband? Bart.' Ian did not hesitate to name him, he might learn more yet.

'Yes. Him.' A cloud of what Ian could only imagine to be fumes from burning manure enveloped his head as Tom puffed away before waving his pipe in acknowledgement. 'Bart. That's his name. I think he wanted to get back with her. It's only an idea, mind, but why else would he be taking her presents? Anyway, she told me he'd called round to see if she'd change her mind about the divorce.'

'Saw her often, did he?' There was a twinkle in Tom's eyes as he realized he was being questioned, albeit subtly.

'Dunno, really. Couple of times a year maybe. She never really said, just that she saw him now and again. Do you think it was him that done it, then? He didn't look the sort to me.' Ian left that particular remark unchallenged. To be fair, Tom was usually a good judge of character but he'd only set eyes on the man once. Besides, as Ian knew only too well, murderers look just like anyone else.

The jumbo sausage arrived, slotted into half a french stick, the onions oozing out on to the plate. The Chief opened it up, smothered one half of the bread with mustard then bit into it with relish, not noticing the grease which dripped on to the end of his tie. Moira would notice though. As he ate, his mind worked. Tom remained silent in deference to a man's enjoyment of his food.

What was puzzling him was that neither of the Barfoots discussed the obvious fact that Henderson was still in touch with his wife. What was it the Reverend said? That she hardly ever saw him. Whatever that might mean. But why should Mrs Henderson conceal his visits from Susan Barfoot, yet be prepared to confide this knowledge to Tom Prendergast? The news meant a third trip to the vicarage was necessary. This was not the first thing Mrs Barfoot had held back on unless, of course, she really didn't know. Maybe the shock was playing tricks with her memory; Ian did not think he'd ever seen a whiter face than hers both times he called on her. Meanwhile he was fortunate enough to be in possession of a vital piece of information gleaned at the very time he was on his way to see a man whose innocence was very much in question, because Bart Henderson, in his statement, said he saw his wife 'some time ago.' The Chief had taken this to mean months rather than weeks. 'Damn and blast it,' he silently rebuked himself, 'a rookie would know better than that. I've done what I keep telling everyone else not to do, worked on an assumption.' He ate the last of his meal and swallowed the remaining two inches of beer. As he placed his pint mug on the table he saw the stain on his tie where it rested on the beginnings of a paunch. He felt guilty and annoyed at the same time. Guilty because of the forbidden calories he'd consumed and annoyed because he had not questioned the words of Bart's statement. The food lay heavy on his stomach as he retraced his steps to the police station. The day was only half over and worse was yet to come.

He went to the incident room to collect his mac and his briefcase as he intended going straight home to Belmont Terrace on his return from Saxborough where, hopefully, he would be able to spend at least some of the evening with his family.

'I'm off now,' he said to the men seated at the desk coordinating statements, 'you know where to find me if I'm needed.' But before he reached the door the telephone rang. Only calls directly connected with the case were supposed to be put through to the incident room. The two PCs were working at the far end of the table and as Ian was nearest, he decided to take the call. He picked up the receiver and was completely taken aback when he heard Moira's voice.

'Ian,' she said, 'I know you're very busy and this couldn't have happened at a worse time, but you couldn't come home for half an hour, could you? Mark's been caught shoplifting.'

SIX

NEITHER GRAHAM nor Laura Sutcliffe was best pleased to learn they were to spend part of their Saturday afternoon down at the local police station. Graham, when not playing golf, went to the club just the same and got his entertainment at the nineteenth hole before returning home to read. Laura was brought up to consider Saturday afternoons were there for the single purpose of providing several hours in which to prepare oneself for whatever social function she was either giving or attending in the evening. It came as quite a shock when the telephone message was received requesting their presence.

'What on earth can they want with us now?' she asked Graham. 'For my part I've told them everything I know.' She stressed the last but one word, implying her husband might not have done likewise. 'We can hardly refuse I suppose.' Laura went upstairs to change, wondering what would pass as suitable attire for the occasion. She chose a dark linen suit and a crisp white blouse and felt she looked rather more like a barrister than a suspect.

As she applied her make-up she noticed a few extra lines under her eyes, no doubt caused by last night's disturbed sleep. She awoke during the early hours with a start. She had been dreaming of Julia. She was alone in the king-size bed she and Graham normally shared, for the sake of appearances, although now Johnny was to move into his own place as soon as he returned from his honeymoon, she intended to put an end to the charade. Unable to go back to sleep she went downstairs to make a hot drink.

While the kettle was boiling she lit a cigarette, then, while she sipped the tea, a second which she knew would not help. She had read somewhere that smokers take longer to fall asleep. Perhaps it was true. It was then the dream came back to her. It was so vivid she was unsure at first whether it was a dream. It was an extension of her telephone conversation with Caroline and she was beginning to believe she was married to a murderer. Had Caroline hinted as much or was it her own thoughts which were responsible for the idea? Whichever way, the idea was not as repugnant to Laura during those early morning hours as it would have been to most people. If Graham was imprisoned for life, which is what she supposed the sentence would be, she would lose nothing and could carry on living as she now did without his annoying presence. She was not *au fait* with his business ventures but knew that as long as goods continued to be manufactured, firms, like her husband's would be required to transport or ship those goods. Besides, Johnny was on the Board, he would see she was well looked after. In fact she might even be better off. Graham's Rover could go for a start, as could the flat in London, the freehold on which should fetch quite a lot.

She had stubbed out her cigarette, knocking the ashtray to one side with a start. What on earth was she thinking? She had Graham tried and convicted without a shred of evidence and was planning a life without him. She softened and, totally out of character, began to feel sorry for him. She asked herself why, if she felt so little for him, didn't she leave. He would still provide for her. Maybe it was because she would miss the life style; a divorced woman didn't have quite the same clout in the community.

Surprised at her initial callous feelings, Laura returned to bed. Graham, presumably, had taken himself off to one of the spare rooms. He did so occasionally if he, too, was unable to sleep. He was able to read there without the light disturbing her.

'Are you ready?' Laura asked, now immaculate in grey and white. 'We might as well get it over with.' They left the house together, Laura wondering if the next few hours would change the course of her life.

The Rover purred into a parking space marked 'Staff Only'. Graham got out and went round to open the door for his wife. Walking the few yards to the entrance, Laura took his arm possessively, as if they were the happiest couple imaginable. Anyone might be watching from all those windows; whatever happened she was determined to put on a good show. Graham ignored the gesture but made no effort to remove her hand. To their indignation they were asked to take a seat. Sergeant Swan was busy at the moment but would be with them shortly.

They were kept waiting for fifteen minutes. Barry decided this was long enough for them to become anxious about the reason for their presence, long enough for the tension to build up which might loosen one of their tongues. 'Surely,' Graham asked himself as they waited, 'Laura hasn't got anything to do with this?' The idea seemed highly unlikely, but on the other hand he knew his wife would go to great lengths to get what she wanted. 'And it's a shame,' he thought sadly, 'she's never really wanted me.' He remembered when they were first married, when she was quite keen on what he referred to as the bedroom stakes. He was aware he was not particularly imaginative but he was Laura's first lover and at the time she appeared satisfied. But when Johnny was born she delayed the moment when he was allowed to return to her bed for as long as she dared. But things had changed; when he made love to her, her lack of interest was obvious. With hindsight he realized her initial enthusiasm was absolutely typical; she played along until she conceived the child she desperately wanted.

Then, when Johnny was about three, Laura decided it was time he had a sibling. Graham recalled the flimsy nightdresses that made a reappearance and the coy remarks at bedtime. But there were no more children. Laura began to talk of adoption. He could not remember being bothered either way but was persuaded it was the right thing to do. It would be good for Johnny and give an unwanted child a home, and, she explained crossly, if they were to stand any chance at all he had to change his attitude, the officials concerned would not consider a half-hearted applicant. Over the following months they were vetted and inspected and no sooner had the papers been signed than the small bundle arrived which, for a short time, disrupted the routine. Graham now had a daughter and her name was Maria.

To his astonishment he allowed the same process to be repeated two years later. He now had a son and two daughters. This child's name was Charmian. Laura had all she wanted and therefore no further need for a husband, especially one who she said slobbered and sweated when they had sex, and who ruined her expensive hairdos. Graham was hurt and embarrassed by these words and rarely bothered to make advances. However, once he was used to the idea, he never regretted taking on this ready-made family. When the girls were small they filled the house with noise and laughter and, unlike their mother, were always affectionately glad to see him. A wave of nostalgia rolled over him as he thought of the evenings when he returned from work and Maria and Charmian would vie for his attention, trying to climb up his legs. Once seated he would take one on each knee and they would smother him in kisses. Later, during their early teens, he suffered doubt at the wisdom of adopting girls, their clothes and boyfriends seemed to infiltrate every corner of the house. When they left home he found he missed them dreadfully. Maria was a qualified nurse in London and judging by her letters was always going to parties in the Nurses' Home. Charmian took a commercial course and had recently been promoted to personal secretary to the managing director of a firm in Ipswich. Her life was as hectic as her sister's, as she shared a flat with two other girls. He went to see them both as often as he could and they were genuinely pleased to see him, but they rarely came home, using their busy lives as an excuse. Whereas Johnny had never shown the slightest indication of leaving his comfortable home. The boy had a lot of his mother in him, he was a cold fish. Graham hoped this was not his fault. He tried his best with him, but as an only child himself and having had little to do with children, was only able to emulate his own father's example and brought him up 'to be a man'. It was too late to worry now, Johnny was twenty-five and a married man. Besides, Laura had indulged him enough to counteract his strictness. It was typical of him that he chose to marry someone so like his mother; no doubt he felt it was the easiest way, there would be no great adjustments to make. Helen was very attractive and could be really charming but underneath there was nothing but ice.

'I'm sorry to have kept you waiting, would you like to come through?' Barry was the model of politeness, although he made no apology for the room into which they were ushered. Beneath a 150-watt bulb, set into the ceiling and shaded only by a metal grill, stood a table and four chairs. On the table was a notebook and a biro.

'Do sit down,' he said, indicating the scuffed, wooden seats. For a moment Barry thought Mrs Sutcliffe was going to wipe hers with a handkerchief before doing so.

'I apologize for bringing you here on a Saturday, but in this job every day is the same, and there are a few points we'd like to clear up. Oh, by the way,' he threw in casually, as a uniformed PC silently joined them, taking his place to one side of the door as if to prevent their escape, 'this is Police Constable Sampson.'

Mrs Sutcliffe might have decided to put on a good show, Barry thought, for he had watched the touching scene of her taking her husband's arm, through the window of the incident room, but the one he had prepared was more than capable of matching it. There were more comfortable surroundings he could have chosen for the interview and, strictly, there was no need for Sampson to be present, he wasn't taking a formal statement, but he was aware these two factors were producing the required amount of intimidation. To be fair, he amended, almost everyone that was brought to this room felt that way.

'I've been going over your statements.' In unison the Sutcliffes stiffened. 'And,' he continued after a well-timed pause, 'everything seems to tie up.' It was comical, the visible easing of tension. Graham even went so far as to run his fingertips over his brow as if he was sweating. 'But what struck me as rather strange was that if you knew Mrs Henderson well enough to have her to dinner...I know,' he interrupted as Laura started to remind him it was ages since she had done so, 'and well enough to invite her to your son's wedding, or rather, for you, sir, to have invited her, why is it that neither of you can recall one single thing pertaining to the lady other than that she was present on the day? Because you see in my experience, when a person feels strongly about another person, one way or the other, they tend to notice what that someone else is doing. I'd like you both to go over the events again and see if anything comes to mind now you've had a day to think about it.' Barry addressed this speech to a spot on the blank wall behind their heads, choosing not to give anything away by making eye contact. He hoped the unfamiliar and to some extent frightening, surroundings would work their usual magic on sluggish memories. They did. It was Laura who responded first.

'Now that you mention it, Sergeant Swan, there was something.' How many times, Barry wondered, had revelations been prefaced with that same phrase? 'As you kindly pointed out, it was not myself, but my husband who invited Julia.' Graham sighed. He could see he was not going to be let off lightly. 'But I am speaking the truth when I say *I,* and I stress the word I, had no contact with her for a long time. Nor did I speak to her at the wedding.' She delivered this little speech with all the pomposity she could muster. 'It might not mean a thing but I did notice Julia deep in conversation with Gerry Clayton. Perhaps you've spoken to him already and know what it was about. He's an ex-teacher, he works for Dennis, Dennis Morley that is, now. That's strange, he and his wife weren't on the guest list either.' She looked pointedly at Graham. 'Unless you invited them too.'

Enough was enough. 'Don't be so bloody stupid, woman. Dennis asked them, he told me a few days before. And Clayton's wife's name, by the way, is Ann. Dennis is a good chap. He thought as they were new here it would be a good way for them to meet people and he knew they'd fit in all right, they're both well educated.' He felt like kicking himself for saying that, it made him sound like a snob, but the interview, and Laura, were putting him on edge.

'Thank you, sir. You were saying, Mrs Sutcliffe?' Barry's manners remained immaculate.

'Yes. Ann Clayton then.' The sarcasm was lost on Barry. He was not aware that it was one of Laura's less endearing habits to call people she considered her social inferiors by a name only similar to the one they possessed. In the short time of their acquaintance she missed on calling Mrs Clayton Angela. 'She was over at the buffet table with Caroline Morley when Gerry excused himself and went across to Julia. I rather got the impression they were having some sort of argument. Julia was extremely flushed and kept shaking her head. Then she upped and left the room.'

'How long was she missing?'

'Oh, hardly any time at all. Long enough to have gone to the bathroom maybe. After that she spent most of the evening with Susan Barfoot.'

For one who claimed to have been barely aware of the victim's presence, Mrs Sutcliffe was giving a good impression of being highly observant. Unless, as the Chief always drummed into them, she was lying.

There was no reason why Clayton and Mrs Henderson should not have conversed, perfectly natural under the circumstances. They had known each other for a couple of weeks, had shared a meal in a restaurant; it would be more unusual if they ignored each other. But, taking into account the allegation they might have been quarrelling, that the quarrel took place out of the hearing of Clayton's wife and that his fingerprints were in Mrs Henderson's house, and adding to that the circumstances of his resignation from his teaching post, Barry was more certain than ever that his gut feeling as to the man's guilt was more than simply a hunch.

'Well I might as well admit it, I talked to Julia too. I didn't say so before because I thought you only wanted to know if we saw or heard anything unusual.' Their brief chat was irrelevant, but he wanted to bring it up before Laura did. 'We discussed the weather, how lucky Johnny and Helen were to have a break in the showers at the time the pictures were being taken and how beautiful Helen looked. Julia was charming as ever and looked well. That was about eight, wasn't it, darling?' Graham was quietly beginning to take his revenge. 'If you remember you weren't terribly happy about me talking to her. In fact, you were rather unpleasant about it at the time. What was it you called her? A slut, I think it was. Not a very nice moment as you can imagine, sergeant.'

Laura was no longer intimidated by her surroundings, her fury at Graham overruled everything. How dare he make a fool of her in front of this nobody.

'Don't think I don't know what you're trying to do,' she said, her voice tight with the effort of trying not to shout. 'Yes. Of course I remember. And at the time you accused me of being a jealous bitch—you forgot to mention that. And, yes, you were right, I was jealous and I'm not afraid to admit it. Who wouldn't be, knowing their husband had slept with her?' Both men saw how much pride it cost her to make that admission and Barry decided to let them argue it out. Who knew what might be learned if they lost their tempers.

'But I did not kill her.' Barry believed her.

Graham said nothing, but paled as if the venom in her words had entered his bloodstream. It was not his intention to cast suspicion upon her, he merely wanted to put her in her place. He had failed in this, as in all things where she was concerned. Didn't she know that beneath the self-protective layers of defence he'd built up over the years he still cared about her? Probably, he decided, still loved her? The affair with Julia and one or two occasional dallyings in London would not have occurred if things were different at home. When they arrived at the police station and Laura had taken his arm he was afraid to show recognition of her touch, had not wanted to put her off; he thought it was a sign they would see the afternoon through together, on the same side for once. How wrong could he be?

'Yes. I knew all along what was going on between you and I hated her. I admit there were times when I wished her dead, but I didn't do it.' Laura's fury subsided, but only temporarily. Barry decided to push the point.

'Didn't you, Mrs Sutcliffe?' Laura felt as if she was in the middle of a nightmare from which she could not wake.

'No. But there are other motives apart from jealousy as you well know. What about greed? Who benefits now she's dead? Or,' she added, grinning maliciously at Graham, 'how about the big one, that highly regarded possession, the male ego? Try that one.' Colour returned to her face. She was going to show these bastards.

'Would you mind clarifying that statement, madam?' Barry asked, guessing she was referring to Graham's discovery that his son was probably screwing the same woman. But he wanted to hear her say it, not out of prurient curiosity, but because he knew the bullocking he was in for if he made assumptions.

ON SATURDAY AFTERNOON Ann Clayton took the car and drove herself to Ipswich. During the long, sleepless night she had made a decision and although she knew they couldn't really afford it she was going to buy something new to wear and have her hair done. For far too long she had worn the same shoulderlength bob; it was time for something more daring.

She was not sure of the motives behind this unusual streak of extravagance but suspected they were a cross between trying to cheer herself up and the belief that if she made more effort with her appearance Gerry would not be tempted to stray again. She knew he was attracted to Julia, impossible for a man to remain untouched by her beauty but—and she didn't think she was kidding herself—it had gone no further than that. As for the fingerprints, there must be a logical reason for their existence; it was just that for the moment she couldn't think of one.

Eventually she found a parking space in a multi-storey car-park, locked the car and headed for the town centre hoping the hairdresser's was not too difficult to find. She had picked it at random from *Yellow Pages.* It was not a good idea to buy the dress first, it might not suit her once her hair was transformed into the wild, red curls she envisaged. Arriving with ten minutes to spare she picked up a magazine and waited in happy anticipation for her turn to be shampooed.

Gerry's hours at the farm were becoming erratic, not that he objected. He worked whenever he was needed and took time off when things were quiet. This Saturday he had all to himself and he looked forward to it. Although he hated shopping he volunteered to go into Ipswich with Ann. She was surprised and pleased and guessed his offer was a way of making up for what she'd been through because of him, but she'd turned him down. She wanted her appearance to be a total surprise. Once she'd left, Gerry flicked on the television but he felt too restless to settle down and watch a film and he was not interested in sport. He picked up one of the books Ann brought him back from the library but it did not hold his interest. He knew then how much he missed teaching. Since his resignation his interest in literature had evaporated, as if he feared reminders of a more academic life. The decorating was complete, likewise the garden. There was nothing more to do outside until the end of the month when they would begin choosing bedding plants.

Gerry was not a man who suffered from boredom, but that's what he put his restlessness down to, not wishing to admit it was this thing hanging over his head crippling his concentration. If only it was all over.

He opened the patio doors and went outside to kick a few loose chippings off the crazy paving and, deciding the weather looked reasonable, thought a walk might do him good, burn up some of his nervous energy. It was overcast with a touch of dampness in the air, but mild enough.

He went inside to fetch a light zipper jacket, locked up and walked down behind the backs of the houses in Ash Farm Road, using a gap in the lattice-work fence the builders had erected when the estate was new as a short cut. Various small boys had rearranged the slats for their own convenience. Once out and on to the country lane running parallel with his own road he was soon past the ugly vista of the industrial estate which lay to the right. He turned into Deben Lane, which was more like the scenery they envisaged when they decided to move to Rickenham. With room for only two cars, and too many bends to allow for overtaking, the road was rarely used. Modern motors preferred the speed of the by-pass. At the end of the lane was a river which ran from its source, the Deben, across country, under the bridge at the top of the High Street and along here to the meadow. He was ashamed to admit he still did not know its name.

Twenty minutes later Gerry rounded the corner on the last stretch of tree-lined road alongside the meadow before entering a side street of terraced houses which led into the town proper. Even from there the only visible sight that the area might be populated was the tall spire of St Luke's, the pinnacle of which was apparently balancing low-hanging banks of cloud equally on either side. The high hedges and a row of poplars planted long ago as a wind-break hid the new office blocks which sprang up at regular intervals and remained empty for months, or even years. Also hidden behind the trees were the lower, corrugated roofs of the units of a second industrial estate, now pretentiously and unoriginally renamed the Poplars Business Park.

A few minutes later Gerry was in the town, opposite the church and the vicarage. At close quarters the clouds no longer appeared to rest on the spire and to the west he saw a patch of widening blue sky. Suddenly a few rays of sunshine bounced off the last roofs of the council houses and momentarily turned them silver. The sight took him by surprise.

He decided the walk had not helped after all. He still felt restless. More than anything else he wanted Julia's murder solved, the person responsible behind bars, even if that person was himself. There were times over the past three years when he found it difficult to differentiate between reality and fantasy, like the time he was accused of having sex with Tina Hutchinson.

Had that really happened? Yes, he believed so. How could he have been so stupid?

But he knew, had known for some time from the way she always sat at the front of his classes and contemplated him from under her long lashes, what she was about. There were times when it was hard to keep his mind on the 'A' level curriculum when she deliberately hitched her uniform skirt over at the waist so that when she crossed her legs he had an unimpeded view of her thighs. She was attractive in the way only eighteen-year-old girls can be, fresh with the bloom of youth.

It was a mistake to offer her a lift home but at the time he felt he had no choice. She had stepped out in front of his car as he was pulling away from his allocated space outside the main school building and he had to break suddenly to avoid hitting her. He managed to stop in time and she leaned forward to brace herself against the blow. He was shaken and assumed Tina was too. The decent thing was to take her home. It did not cross his mind until much later to wonder what she was doing in the car-park in the first place. All the pupils left by the main gates to catch their buses or to walk home.

But somewhere between the school and her home she persuaded him she was perfectly all right and as she was not expected home until later why didn't they go for a drive? Alone with her for the first time, the smell of her young skin filling the car, he agreed. But where they went and exactly what happened he could not recall. That was what worried him most. Whoever had seduced whom and what he felt at the time was irrelevant, the memory was gone. As part of his

Dip. Ed. he read some psychology and wondered if he was using a mental defence mechanism to block out that hour and a half. Dissociation, for example, where inconsistencies in thought and conduct could be over-looked. The knowledge that his behaviour was un-professional, coupled with a hidden desire for a repeat performance, might have created such a gap. That was why, at the time he did not—could not—defend him-self. His only solution was to leave teaching alto-gether, that way there was no temptation. As to the other allegations, he was positive there was nothing in them. He did touch girls on occasion, it was unavoid-able, but nothing sexual was meant by his gestures. Because of these sordid accusations he now avoided physical contact, a quick handshake was the most he permitted himself. Even with Ann he was less loving, but she understood. He was lucky to have her, a lot of women would have left.

A memory stirred. Julia. He had touched Julia, he could still feel the warmth of her under his hand. They were walking back from the Feathers, the three of them, the first time they met. There was a queue of jostling teenagers waiting outside the cinema for the afternoon performance of the latest science fiction film. Two of them accidentally bumped into Julia knocking her off the pavement. Instinctively he grabbed her arm to pull her out of the road and she was soft and feminine, and certainly desirable. But had he touched her since?

Gerry was startled to find he was gripping the gate in front of St Luke's, beads of sweat standing out on his forehead. 'Yes,' he thought, 'I could have done it, maybe during one of those periods I can't remember.

I could have made love to her, then killed her.' After all, his fingerprints were there as evidence. But Ann provided his alibi. Without hesitation she told the police how they left the reception together and were kindly given a lift home by people they were introduced to that evening and who happened to live near them. That much he could remember and anyway, the police had checked and verified this. Once home, Ann made coffee and while they drank it they talked of general things as people who have been married ten years and have spent an evening out together do. Then they went to bed. Together. They had always shared the same bed even during those awful weeks prior to his resignation. In the morning they woke to the sound of the alarm clock, a fact they both remembered as they argued briefly over whose fault it was the damn thing had been set at all. Sunday was a day when there was no rush to get off to work. But the police were interested in the intervening hours. Was there any way in which he could have left the house, walked the short distance to Julia's house and killed her? Ann was not a light sleeper—if he got up in the night to have a pee she hardly stirred—but surely, even in sleep, she would have noticed his prolonged absence. Gerry needed someone to talk to, someone other than a policeman or his wife, an objective ear to pour his troubles into. Perhaps the thought had been in his subconscious all along for in front of the gate on which he was leaning was what surely must be a refuge, the vicarage.

He made his way through the small churchyard which had been filled long ago. All burial now took place at the cemetery on the main road. Entering the vicarage garden by the gate which connected it to the churchyard he noticed a car parked on the drive, so presumably somebody was in. Gerry was not a religious man but he had nowhere else to turn and at that moment he was prepared to take any sort of comfort offered. Susan, or her husband, would listen to him without censure.

He walked round to the front of the house. The door stood open and he nearly changed his mind. He heard a voice, raised shrilly in anger, and surprise replaced self-pity. He stepped nearer and coughed, not wishing to cause embarrassment. Never in all his years as a teacher had he seen anyone walloped like this. Susan was clutching a large adolescent by the arm and inflicting blow after blow across his legs and buttocks with a floury rolling-pin held in her other hand. The boy, more than big enough to look after himself, barely struggled. He made no sound and his face registered total shock.

'Mrs Barfoot,' Gerry said loudly, no longer concerned about any embarrassment. 'Susan.' She whirled round, releasing Matthew, her naturally pale face blotchy and red, her lips pinched, as he stepped uninvited into her hall. At that moment she was ugly.

'Gerry, it's you,' she said breathlessly, brushing a hand through her hair. Matthew remained where he was with a look in his eye Gerry could not interpret. Susan remembered his presence.

'Go to your room, Matthew. I'll speak to you later. Come in, won't you?' Matthew, aware the ordeal was over, went upstairs. At the top he paused and said quietly, but audibly, 'I deserved it, you know.'

So that's what was written on his face. Satisfaction. 'I can see I've come at a bad time.' It was a feeble comment to make after what he'd just witnessed but he was lost for words. He knew he wasn't going to find the comfort he sought there either. He was disappointed but knew it to be selfish to unburden himself on a woman who was going through a domestic crisis herself, but he felt an obligation to stay, at least until she was calmer, for the sake of the boy. He felt slightly nauseous at the thought she might be one of those women who consistently beat their children. And if she was, he wondered what he could do about it.

'No, it's all right,' Susan was saying. 'I could do with a cup of tea.' She could not let him go now. He was bound to mention what he'd seen to someone. She could not envisage remaining in Rickenham if her husband's parishioners believed she hit her children. Better to let him hear the truth about Matthew than think badly of her.

'Are you sure?'

'Yes, positive. Come on through.' And then something was released in Susan. She was unable to stop the flow of the tears which filled her eyes; racking sobs shook her body. 'I'm sorry, I'm sorry,' she stammered, 'it's been such an awful week. First Julia and now this. Oh, Gerry, what on earth must you think of me?' He put an arm around her shoulder, a perfectly natural gesture, but immediately dropped it to his side again. No, he must not touch anyone.

Somehow they'd got themselves into the kitchen. Susan blew her nose, sniffed and tried to pull herself together. 'I've never smacked either of them before, you know. I don't know what came over me. That poor boy, whatever must he be feeling? Do you think I should go up to him?'

'No, leave him for a while, he'll be all right.' Gerry believed her; by the look on Matthew's face he was sure he'd never been subjected to such treatment before. The boy would be feeling hurt and very angry, he would need time to himself to settle down.

Susan filled the kettle but could not complete the task of making tea. She sat at the kitchen table, head in her hands and was disgusted to feel the tears starting again. Gerry let her cry, probably the best thing for her. There was a box of pastel-coloured tissues next to the toaster, he grabbed a handful and handed them to her. 'Here,' he said, 'I'll make the tea.' If he couldn't be tactile he could at least do something useful. Glancing round he saw the necessary equipment, all beautifully clean. The stainless steel kettle gleamed, unlike his own at home which frequently had spots of bacon fat or a few sticky coffee granules stuck to its surface. Spooning tea into the pot Gerry, not always the most sensitive of men, realized there was no chance of confiding in Susan Barfoot today.

'I'm awfully sorry, Gerry, putting you to all this trouble, I'm not normally like this, but ever since, well ever since I heard about Julia nothing seems right any more. I miss her so much. We were the best of pals, you know.' There were still a few tears on her cheeks but through them she managed to summon up a wan smile, a little-girl-lost expression in her eyes. And a little girl was what she reminded Gerry of. Chatting in the supermarket he was not able to put his finger on it—there was something about her—but seeing her today he recognized it, it was in the way she acted, even down to the outdated schoolgirl expressions she sometimes used. But there was more to it than that: it was as if, in a crowd, she was able to convey the impression she was an adult who has her life under control, someone who was able to cope efficiently and calmly with any situation which arose. Obviously this was not the case. And the other thing—perhaps his male ego was working overtime—on the few occasions they met he got the impression she fancied him. Even now he was getting those vibes. He tried to concentrate on what she was saying.

'I don't know what to do. I thought I'd made a good job of bringing up the boys. I just can't understand it.' More tears hovered but now she blinked them firmly away. The red blotches had faded and once more Susan gave the impression of being a dainty, but very much alive, doll.

'I lost my temper, not something I'm prone to, and I should've talked to Matthew, let him explain, instead of laying into him like that. He was caught shoplifting, he and a friend. I handled it badly, I should have sent him to his room and waited until I was calmer or Michael came home, he's very good in situations like this.' This was more like it, the sort of problem Gerry was also good at dealing with. He was used to sitting with parents and listening while they spoke of their children's predicaments. Sometimes they blamed themselves, sometimes their children's friends or the school. More often than not these things turned out to be a single incident of theft, performed out of daring or rebellion and were only occasionally the beginning of a criminal career.

'A lot of kids do it,' he told her gently, falling back into the old role with ease. 'It doesn't necessarily mean anything. Probably a bit of a dare. Were the police involved?'

Susan's laugh was cynical.

'It depends what you mean. But no further action's going to be taken. You see Mark was with him, the Detective Chief Inspector's son. Oh, it'll be hushed up all right.'

Gerry asked himself if there was any getting away from the man.

'Where was it? Which shop?'

'The newsagent's in Brett Avenue. Why?'

'Well quite often when it's a small business they don't prosecute, there's no need, they probably know the parents and have a quiet word. Was it sweets they took?' Susan nodded. 'Yes, usually is, and the kids rarely have the nerve to go back again. I don't think there's anything much to worry about. Have a word with him, you and Michael. He's probably terrified about what's going to happen to him, that'll be punishment enough.'

'Thanks, Gerry. You don't know how much it's helped, having someone to talk to. Michael won't be back for a while yet. And thank God you arrived when you did.' Susan was her usual pale self again, shaken with the knowledge that had he not come when he did she might have seriously harmed her son. She rose, placing a hand on his shoulder as she saw he was about to do likewise. 'No, stay for a while. I'm fine now. I'll make some more tea and you can tell me why you came.'

His mood of anxiety, near panic, no longer existed. Witnessing someone else's distress and being able to help alleviate it had distracted him temporarily. He had lost the urge to discuss his own problems so instead he used the excuse that he came to offer a dinner invitation, saying he and Ann wanted to repay the kindness shown them since their move. He hoped Susan was too wrapped up in her own thoughts to appreciate he and Michael had only spoken on two occasions.

'That's very kind of you. I'll have to check with Michael first, he's always so busy, as you can imagine. I'll have to let you know.' But she had no intention of telling Michael. For a start she did not think he would be keen to go after their conversation of the previous Sunday but, more importantly, despite her outwardly hospitable manner towards him, she never wanted to set eyes on Gerry Clayton again if she could possibly help it.

Just then she would have been unable to say why. It was much later, when it was all over, that she knew the reasons. And as for hitting Matthew, it was not the shoplifting episode which caused that outburst. It was something far worse.

IAN DROPPED HIS BRIEFCASE heavily on to the table. 'Yes,' he said, 'yes,' unsure whether his affirmations meant he was busy or he would go home. What a time for a thing like this to happen. What a choice to have to make. Duty to the force, the public and the murdered woman, or duty to his wife and son? Neither Mark nor Moira was injured or in danger but neither was he indispensable. Henderson could wait. For once he was going to put his family first. It was, he recognized with a jolt, the first time he had done so.

'Something's cropped up. Get...no, on second thought, ring Henderson and tell him I can't make it. Ask him to come here. Tomorrow. About eleven. I'll see him then.' Maybe it was not such a bad thing after all. The man was already on tenterhooks. When he discovered there was no urgency after all, that he was being trusted to turn up, he would relax. 'And when suspects think the pressure is off they're more likely to sing,' Ian told himself, although he guessed he was still trying to convince himself he was doing the right thing.

'Right, sir. Will you be back later?' PC Welland said.

'I'm not sure at the moment. You can get me at home.'

Ian threaded his way through the Saturday afternoon traffic. The pavements were crowded. Women carried bags and pushed prams, small children hanging on to the handles. Groups of schoolchildren hung around outside fast food outlets, dropping their litter on the streets as if wastebins had not yet been invented. Ian was furious and nearly pulled into the side of the road to have a word with a boy who chucked a Kentucky Fried Chicken box at the wheels of his car. What sort of parents let their kids behave in such a way? Then he remembered the purpose of his journey. But Mark was different. Mark was his son. And look what he'd done, what kind of parent did that make him?

The drive home took almost twice as long as usual. There was a queue waiting for space in the inadequate car-park next to the supermarket which held up the flow of traffic round the new roundabout, a useless so-called improvement in Ian's opinion. A bus pulled alongside him as he waited, the rhythmic throb of its diesel engine loud, the fumes filling his car. He wound up the window, cursing Saturdays, traffic, murderers and children. At least Moira would have some support when she needed it. There were enough men working on the case and look at Harry Watkins, he knew for a fact that the man took all the off duty due to him and spent most of it with his family and this did not prevent him from being one of the best detectives he'd ever known, with a smaller percentage of un-solved crimes on his books than most divisions. Which reminded him, he ought to let Harry know he wasn't coming.

'Ian, thank you. I'm so glad you're here,' Moira said as she opened the door on hearing the car pull into the drive. 'Mark's upstairs. I don't know what to say to him. I didn't expect...' Ian dropped his car keys on to the telephone table and put his arms around her. She was fifteen years his junior and now, seeing her without make-up, tears in her eyes, she managed to look younger than that. It was unfair, he thought, as he handed her his handkerchief, worry aged him but had the opposite effect on his wife.

'Come on, let's have a word with him.' Together they went upstairs. Mark was lying on his bed, he was scared, his heart thudding painfully in his chest, but a belligerent scowl hid his feelings from his parents.

'What's it all about then, Mark? Did someone put you up to it?' Mark shook his head, disgusted that his father didn't even think him capable of doing this without someone else giving him the idea.

'I always thought we gave you enough pocket money. We increase it every so often. Was that it? Didn't you have enough money?' The scowl deepened.

'For God's sake answer me, boy. I can't help you if you won't talk to me.'

Mark sat up. He'd had enough. Talk to him? How many times in the past had he tried? It wouldn't do any good, he could talk all day and Dad wouldn't listen. 'Aren't you going to arrest me then? I thought that was your job? That's what you do with criminals, isn't it?'

'You're not a criminal, you've just acted like a stupid kid, that's all.' Ian knew this was not going well. His temper was getting the better of him, not because of Mark's misdemeanour but because of his attitude. He had expected some sign of contrition or maybe an apology.

'And how would you know?' Mark shouted. 'You're never here, why should you care how I behave. Anyway, I'm not a kid.'

'Ian.' Moira grabbed his arm. He had taken a menacing step forward and for one awful moment she thought he was going to hit the boy. Ian took a deep breath. His intention had been to sit on the bed beside Mark and try to reason with him; obviously he was not very good at making his intentions clear to his family. But at least he was getting the gist of what this was all about. In future he would have a bit more sympathy for parents who dragged their kids into the police station if they discovered they'd been stealing.

'You're right, son, I'm not at home as often as I should be, or would like to be, but you have to understand that what I do is important. Not more important than you and your mother even if it does appear that way at times. I love you both dearly and I work hard to provide you with the things I think you need, but at the same time, believe it or not, I want to make the world a nicer place, a safer place for people to live in.' What Ian said was true. He knew he was fighting a losing battle but it would not stop him trying, but the words came out wrong. He thought he sounded like a pompous do-gooder. The trouble was, at work he was articulate, able to ask a leading question without making it appear so. He could hear what was left unsaid as well as what was spoken, whereas at home he wanted to relax. He should not have to be on his toes in his own house. His anger rose again. And why was he standing there having to explain all this to a fourteen-year-old boy whose behaviour that day could hardly be called exemplary?

Moira looked from her husband to her son. Yes, there were going to be problems there, and sooner than she anticipated. Both wore the same stubborn expression, brows furrowed, lips set. She saw what they didn't: they were very similar in temperament. It was time to intervene.

'Are you going back to work, Ian?'

The question threw him. 'I didn't intend to. Why?'

'And you, Mark? Are you going to lie there sulking all afternoon? Because,' she continued without waiting for further answers, 'I'm not going to have my Saturday afternoon ruined by either of you. I'm going to make some coffee and I suggest, if either of you has any sense, you join me and we'll discuss this like sensible people.'

It was unlike Moira to put her views so forcefully but she achieved what she set out to do: put both Mark and Ian in the wrong and thereby unite them. She left them to it.

Father and son's eyes met. The look they gave each other contained both anger and something indefinable. 'Here,' Ian said, offering his hand. 'Come on, son, let's go down and talk about it.' Mark hesitated briefly, then took the hand. They found Moira preparing coffee and sandwiches. She knew well enough how to pacify her men.

Gradually, during the course of the afternoon Ian began to get an inkling of what was wrong. For one thing he discovered he had never held a proper conversation with his child. To him, he was just that, his child, and he supposed he would remain one until some unspecified date when he metamorphosed into an adult overnight, ignoring the fact that growing up was a gradual process. Mark's own views on his education, his home life and his future were far more mature than he gave him credit for. Conversely, certain of the things he said proved him still to be a boy.

'It's not that I want you around every minute, Dad. It's just that you *never* seem interested in anything I'm doing. You'd even forgotten I don't like football. And if you were home a lot more I'd still mostly want to go out with my mates. I don't know, I can't explain really.' But Ian understood. He had neglected his son, who was not asking for much, not by his absence, but by not accepting him as an individual. He knew he was often too tired to take in what the boy was saying and that on the rare occasions he did take him anywhere, he did so without taking into account his interests. It was not put into so many words but Ian wondered if the shoplifting incident was a way of gaining his attention. Mark called himself a criminal and Ian spent his time talking to criminals. Simplistic maybe, but it could be true.

'Matthew feels the same,' Mark continued, in full flow now he had his father's undivided attention. 'It wasn't really his fault, he only sugg...' he stopped himself before he gave his friend away, 'he only did it because he's bloody miserable at the moment.' It was the first time Ian had heard his son swear but he decided to let it go for the moment. 'I hope he doesn't get into too much trouble. But his mother's a bit like you, she's always too busy to talk to him. She's forever at these meetings and things and she's not like Mum, she's obsessional. Always cleaning and tidying and won't let him or Josh make any sort of mess.' This was news to Moira but she hid her smile. Her impression was that she never stopped cleaning and tidying.

'Anyway, Matthew says ever since Mrs Henderson died she's got worse. She even threw out all his magazines he was collecting. And he misses Julia a lot. Dad, what's going to happen to us?'

Despite his earlier bravado, Mark was worried. Ian left the answer to Moira. She was the one to receive the telephone call from the newsagent and she was the one who had the embarrassing task of going down there to collect him, arriving only minutes after Susan Barfoot departed with Matthew. Both boys were too scared to make a run for it. Besides, as the newsagent knew their parents, it seemed easier to stay and face the music at once.

'Probably nothing. Mr Cowan has been very reasonable. Because he knows us, and the Barfoots, he guessed you weren't the sort to make a habit of it. As you gave him back what you stole,' she used the word deliberately, 'and apologized, he'll let it go at that. But if he, or anyone else, ever catches you again, it'll be a different story.'

Ian did not see the boy's flush of shame, he was thinking about something he said.

'So Matthew was very fond of Mrs Henderson. Did you know her, Mark?' One more pointer to show how little notice he took of his son. Only recently did he learn he knew Matthew Barfoot, and now it seemed his son also knew the dead woman.

'Not really. Well, a bit I suppose. If we were down by the river and she was out walking she usually stopped for a chat, you know, to ask us what we were doing, like. Not nosy though. And once or twice when it was really cold she asked us in for coffee if we were passing that way.' Mark stopped, wondering if more trouble lay ahead. The only way he and Matthew could be coming from that direction was if they used the gap in the fence. He hoped they weren't to be blamed for that also. But Ian was only interested in what he knew of Mrs Henderson. From the way in which Mark spoke he thought he'd liked her.

'You thought she was OK then? Apart from her not being nosy, what else can you tell me about her?' Mark shrugged and ran a hand nonchalantly through his close-cropped hair, disguising the fact he was secretly delighted to be asked his opinion on something connected with one of his father's cases.

'Well, she worked at home, she showed us some of the things she'd had published, a bit boring really, all about furniture and doing up the bathroom.' Ian did know. There were examples of her work amongst her papers but they were a little more sophisticated than how they had just been described.

'She could tell a good joke, too. I can never re-member the punch lines, and she used to ask me what I'd been doing in Art.' There was more than liking in their relationship, that much was obvious. Ian won-dered if Mark had a crush on her. How old did a boy need to be before he had those feelings? Ian could not remember. And Mark's art. Once or twice he'd cast a perfunctory glance at his drawings and probably made some patronizing remark such as 'very nice'. Could it be his son was in possession of a talent of which he was not aware?

'Dad?'

'Sorry, I was thinking.' He grinned. 'I'm trying hard, you know, not to drift off. It won't be an easy habit to break. Bear with me. Anyway, what I was thinking was that it's a long time since I had a look at your work. Fancy getting it out now?' Moira squeezed his hand, a silent thank you for the effort he was making.

'Yea, sure. Won't be a minute.' He crashed out through the kitchen door—for the past year he seemed unable to do anything quietly—and took the stairs two at a time. He returned with a small portfolio and proudly held out the contents for inspection.

Ian was genuinely surprised at the quality of the drawings and the delicate sketches of wild flowers were beautifully executed. He took his time going through them.

'That's what I want to be, an artist.'

This was news indeed. But what had he expected? His son was still at school, coming up to his mock exams. He did know enough to be aware that Mark would stay on for further education provided his exam results continued to be as good as they were, but he had not thought beyond that time. Yes, what career had he thought his son would pursue?

He turned to the next drawing and received one of the biggest shocks of his life. It was like looking in a mirror.

'When did you do this?'

'Last term sometime.'

'It's very good.' It was. The likeness was uncanny, but did Ian always look as grim as his son had portrayed him?

'It's a hard life, you know, being an artist. You have to be very good to succeed, I believe. Not many do, and of course, I hear it's quite difficult to make a living. You could always teach it.'

Mark was disappointed. 'I don't want to teach, I want to paint. Anyway, Miss Peters thinks I might get a place at a good art college if the standard of my work stays the same.'

'Does she now?' Ian was astonished. At fourteen he had no more idea of what he wanted to do when he left school than any of his classmates. They lived for the holidays. Despite his aversion to school he had achieved a fairly good level of education and gone on to spend a couple of years at technical college. There he discovered he was not cut out to be an artisan. He went from job to job and finally responded to a police recruiting campaign. He enjoyed the life right from the start and never looked back.

'What did you want to know, Dad, about Mrs Henderson?' Mark asked as he packed away his pictures. Ian picked up the threads of their previous conversation; he was miles away, hoping his son would find as much satisfaction in his chosen career as he did.

'Anything you can think of really. For example, did you ever see anyone else at her house when you went there?'

'No, not actually in the house.'

'Outside?'

'Um. A man. He was carrying a big parcel. I don't know who he was but I saw him knock on the door and she let him in.' This seemed to tie in with what Tom Prendergast told him.

'When was this, Mark?'

'On a Sunday, about three weeks ago I think.' Ian had been about to reprimand him for not saying anything before, but why should he? The boy could not know the information might be important. And, had Ian taken more interest, he would have known he knew Mrs Henderson.

'I don't suppose you can remember what he looked like?'

'Oh yes, I can. He was tall, about six foot, and he had on jeans and a checked shirt and an anorak. His hair was sort of sandy coloured and he had a beard. And he had the parcel of course.' Ian grinned. His son had given him a perfect description of Bart Henderson, or if not him, the man whose arm Julia held in the framed wedding photograph pushed beneath some correspondence in her bureau drawer. Mark had obviously inherited his eye for detail. He'd make a terrific policeman. Or a terrific artist.

'You're sure about this?'

'Yep. Certain. Will I have to go to court and say so?' He was excited at the prospect, having no idea what a boring process it usually was.

'Not if I can help it, but you could come down to the station, say after school on Monday, and look through some mug shots, see if you can identify him.'

There was no real necessity for this but it was time to get Mark more involved in his life and vice versa. He could not remember the last time he visited the station but he was certainly much younger and at the time had shown some enthusiasm. His suggestion was rewarded with an uninhibited hug, the first his son had given him for many months.

AT FOUR FIFTEEN, one and a half hours after their arrival, Barry let the Sutcliffes leave. He was wrong in his assumption that more might come to light, the whole thing merely ended in a slanging match, a major domestic dispute maybe, but hardly relevant to the murder. It had all come out, though. Laura admitted she believed Johnny was also seeing 'that whore' as she referred to Julia. They went over their initial statements again but they remained unaltered.

PC Welland put his head round the door of the interview room where Barry was sitting contemplating the wasted time. 'The Chief's gone home. He went some time ago. Some sort of family crisis. D'you know anything about it? He wouldn't go unless it was urgent. Hope nobody's ill. Anything new here?'

'Nope. Nothing new, and no, I don't know why the Chief's gone home. Better get back to this bloody guest list, I suppose.' There were only a few people left to contact, those who had not answered the first time. It shouldn't take more than half an hour. After that he would follow the boss's example and go home. There was a rather sexy brunette who was probably washing her hair right now in anticipation of their date. On the fourth call he wondered whether he'd have to stand her up.

The Richardsons were old friends of the Morleys. They did not know of Julia's death until Barry told them as they had gone to spend the week with relatives in Bath and returned only an hour or so ago. And they knew Mrs Henderson and spoke to her at the reception. Mrs Richardson would make a superb witness in the box, her mind was computer-like in its ability to record, store, then reproduce whole chunks of conversation. She distinctly recalled seeing Julia in what appeared to be a heated discussion with a man whom she described as having greyish hair, worn a little longer than was now fashionable. 'I thought him rather handsome,' she said, 'in a lean and rugged sort of way.' She was, of course, referring to Gerry Clayton and Barry was more than keen to hear anything that pointed a finger towards him.

'Look,' he said, 'I know you've only just travelled back, but would it be possible for me to pop over and see you? Say in half an hour?' It was possible, so Barry went to the incident room to check the large-

scale map on the wall. 'The Graylings,' Little Endes-
ley was the address he was looking for, the village was
a few miles out of Rickenham. Mrs Richardson gave
him directions and told him he couldn't miss it. Barry
knew from experience of the lanes outside the town
that when a person said you couldn't miss it, it invariably meant you did.

'DAD,' Mark said later that evening between the
mouthfuls of lasagne, one of his favourite meals, 'that
man, the one I saw at Mrs Henderson's, I'm not sure,
I mean I couldn't swear to it, but I think I saw him
there again last Sunday.'

'What!'

'You know, before Mum and I went to the beach.
Mum sent me up to the shop for some tomatoes and
when I went past the bottom of Churchill Way I
thought I saw him getting into his car. It looked like
him anyway.'

'What time was it, Mark? Think carefully now.'

'Mum was doing the picnic and we left at eleven, it
must've been about nine thirty.'

'You have earned yourself an extra pound on top of
your pocket money,' Ian told him, forgetting his earlier idea of stopping it altogether for a month.

He rang the station. Henderson had agreed to come
to Rickenham Green the following morning. His instinct had been to have him picked up immediately but
on reflection he decided to interview him at the scene
of the crime. It was, he knew, an unorthodox decision but on the other hand, Mark was not certain it
was the same man.

SEVEN

STRICTLY SPEAKING, Mrs Bedlow was employed for general cleaning and the preparation of an evening meal on weekdays only, but if the Sutcliffes entertained at home on a Saturday or Sunday she helped out, only too glad of the extra money. What with the wedding and a couple of dinner parties, she was beginning to feel as if she lived at Longrove Park. Still, it was easier than being over at the Morleys, for whom she used to work. Not that her tasks differed in any real respect, it was just that Longrove Park was nearer. Apart from not having to get up quite so early she was eighty pence a day better off through the bus fare she saved. To a person in Mrs Bedlow's position those four pounds a week made a considerable difference.

She was not expected on Sunday until six o'clock. The Sutcliffes were lunching with the Morleys but returning in order to host a cocktail party. Rita Bedlow would spend an hour concocting trays of assorted canapés, then leave them in the kitchen for Laura, who would no doubt take the credit for them herself, to hand around. During the morning Rita made a half hearted attempt to clear up after her own untidy family and found it impossible to believe she had once managed in the cramped space when they were all at home. The two oldest boys had left, Samantha and the two youngest remained. Piling a load of her daughter's flimsy underwear into the washing machine she recalled one of the highlights of her job. The wedding last weekend. Although there were many jobs to attend to, jobs she was sure Laura could easily have managed on her own, she had enjoyed it immensely. She was surprised to be asked but the Sutcliffes had invited all their staff, and she accepted with alacrity. Bert, her husband, had made her day when he commented she looked a treat in navy and white, colours she felt no one could go wrong with. To complete the ensemble a matching picture hat was pushed down firmly on her newly blue-rinsed hair.

Rita Bedlow had no qualms about such an event. She knew exactly how to behave at functions—not for nothing had she worked for both families for many years. Helping out at dinner parties she observed table manners and general behaviour and would not have been intimidated by a royal garden party. She had, however, wondered if the members of these families would converse with her. Serving meals at both establishments she was used to being treated as if she was not there, as if being a menial—a word she learned from her son, Derrick, the only one to make it to college—made her invisible and deaf to what was being said, unless the words were addressed to her. Her rotundity belied the former and no one who knew her could accuse her of being deaf. There was very little she missed. At least she knew Mrs Henderson to speak to and that nice Mrs Barfoot and her husband would be there and would ask after her children. 'And speaking of Mrs Henderson,' she said to herself struggling to latch the door of the hard-working washing machine, 'she didn't half put that bloke in his place.' She knew he was the manager at the Morleys' place but she hadn't liked the look of him, he was a bit too—what was the word?—Bohemian, that was it. Another useful word she picked up from Derrick. She thought he was chatting Mrs Henderson up and in Rita Bedlow's eyes only one man was good enough for her and he was married to that bitch Laura. And if she was his wife she'd make sure he got his hair cut; it was over his collar. 'Fancy,' she told herself as she kicked on the switch of the vacuum cleaner, another temperamental piece of equipment, 'carrying on like that when his own wife was in the room, and what a mousy little thing she is.'

Naturally she was disappointed she couldn't see it through to the end but with Bert wanting a bit of supper when he returned from the pub she had to leave at ten, and Bert was not to be trusted to get his own, not with a few drinks inside him; he'd have the whole place alight in no time. Besides, she was supposed to help out again in the morning. All the bedrooms at Longrove Park were being used by wedding guests and they were to be served breakfast before travelling back to their respective homes. At least it would give her a chance for a nice little chat with Maria and Charmian. There was no time to speak to them on the Saturday, with them both being bridesmaids. Yes, all in all it was a most enjoyable day. But what a terrible shock to think Mrs Henderson was dead. It hardly seemed possible.

As she carried the hoover upstairs she thought about the row she overheard between Julia and Gerry Clayton and felt a bit guilty she had not mentioned it to the police but there was no way she was going to say anything against Mrs H, dead or alive. A very nice young man had come to take her statement, but she'd expected that from what she heard at the Sutcliffes'. She made him a cup of tea and thought how pleasant it was not to be discussing Andy or Richard who always seemed to be in some sort of scrape. There was also something else, something which to Rita Bedlow seemed totally irrelevant. To anyone but her who was so used to being up at the crack of dawn, the actions of the person she encountered at six thirty as she made her way to Longrove Park to start frying the bacon would have seemed unusual. Only now, a week later, did the faintest shadow of suspicion cross her mind. Except it was impossible. Rita Bedlow laughed, she must be going daft, it was the most stupid idea she'd had in her life.

But it wasn't, and had she gone straight to the police instead of peeling the potatoes for the Sunday roast, she would have saved Detective Chief Inspector Roper five more days of anxiety.

THE INITIAL IMPETUS of the case was wearing off, it always did. At first the teams of experts did their thing at the scene of the crime, the forensic lot, the plan drawers and the surgeon, then followed a burst of inquiries, door to door and otherwise. All the information was filed, cross-checked and stored, every possible lead or clue looked at from every angle. Then, nothing. People were re-interviewed but time was making the trail stale, what might have been remembered when the news was fresh was forgotten as the days passed. This was the time when they needed to be more alert than usual, the time when lethargy might strike and something vital be confused with the mundane. Everyone on the force was aware of this but it did not prevent it happening.

However, at ten o'clock on Sunday morning, 'I think we've got him,' Barry and Ian spoke almost simultaneously, then stopped and looked at each other in surprise. Barry, because he thought the Chief spent Saturday afternoon at home in the bosom of his family sorting out whatever domestic chaos caused him to leave early, and Ian because Barry could not possibly be in possession of the information supplied by his son.

Ian broke the astonished silence. 'What do you mean? Who?'

'Gerry Clayton, as I said from the start.'

'Sorry to disappoint you old son, it's not him.'

'OK, tell me who you think it is and I'll tell you why you're wrong.'

'It appears,' Ian said with a touch of smugness, 'young Judy Robbins hit the nail on the head when she said to me "cherchez the husband".'

'Oh, come off it, not Bart Henderson.' The disgust in Barry's voice was plain, the disgust and the disappointment. It was bad enough if his hunch was wrong, but worse if that women's libber, Judy Robbins, was right.

'Come on, let's get some of that revolting coffee and see if we can't sort it out. Henderson won't be here for another hour yet.'

They set the polystyrene containers on the table, Barry lit a cigarette and began to recount his conversation with the Richardsons.

Without too much difficulty he had found the cottage where they lived and was welcomed like a long-

lost relative. The Richardsons were that breed of people who had not been, and never would be, on the
wrong side of the law. Consequently they relished an-
swering questions put to them by the police. It made
them feel they were helping the community, doing
their duty as honest citizens.

'You took statements?' Ian wanted to know. Barry
nodded. 'Not alone I hope.' Barry looked at him from
under his eyebrows. Of course not alone, he was a
Detective Sergeant, not some uniformed woodentop.
He had taken a man with him. He did not bother to
enlighten his boss that it only occurred to him as he
was leaving the station and he'd had to return to find
an available man.

'Yes, well,' he continued, 'the Richardsons have
known the Morleys for a long time, and through them,
met the Sutcliffes. They weren't too sure about any
relationship between the deceased and Graham Sutcliffe but had their suspicions something might have
been going on. As they said, it was really none of their
business, but it was the conversation between Clayton and Mrs Henderson I was interested in. They had
overheard it.'

'You'll have to ask my wife about that,' Mr Richardson had said, chuckling as he lit a cigar. 'She has a
photographic memory for such things, if that's the
way to describe it. She remembers all she hears. Means
I can't get away with anything.' Mr Richardson,
though, appeared to be a man who had nothing to
conceal. He was paunchy, relaxed and spoke of his
wife with genuine fondness in his voice. Barry Swan
pictured him as the central figure in a Somerset
Maugham play, sitting on some Eastern veranda, gin

and tonic in his hand. Mrs Richardson was the worldly one.

'I don't actually agree with it myself,' she said, 'but I know nowadays it's quite commonplace for people to have affairs. About Julia and Graham? I really couldn't say for sure, but there was always a certain frisson when they were both in the same room. And, Mr Clayton did you say his name was? Odd really, and it goes to show I may be wrong about Graham, but their conversation struck me as some sort of lovers' quarrel. He was trying to persuade her to let him see her on Sunday, the following day, that is, but she wouldn't have it. She said, and these were her words, "not after what happened last time". Then she said she was expecting a visitor anyway and was not certain what time he would arrive.'

'He?' Barry had asked.

'Oh, yes, she definitely said "he". As I was saying, Mr Clayton was quite persistent, said he really must talk to her. When he wouldn't take no for an answer Julia left the room. She looked near to tears.'

'And that was it?'

'Yes. When Julia came back Mr Clayton was over at the buffet table with a lady I took to be his wife.' Mrs Richardson glanced at Barry and he detected a glint of humour in her eyes, probably the humour which endeared her to her husband, as she said, 'Well, they left together anyway.'

Detective Sergeant Swan and his companion, who had been busy scribbling down the contents of the interview in his notebook, accepted the offer of a cup of tea. More accurately, Barry accepted as it was not up to his subordinate to do so. There were days when he felt he might drown in the stuff, but this was not one of them. There was something about the couple he liked, he found himself easy in their company. Aware that the formal part of the visit was concluded, Mrs Richardson was in no hurry to let her new friends go. She chatted about general matters as they sipped the tea, but with the murder being uppermost in her mind, she could not help reverting back to it and the wedding preceding it.

'Susan Barfoot seemed a bit harassed, don't you think?' she asked her husband apropos of nothing. 'After that little scene between Julia and Mr Clayton she was quite flushed. She was a bit short with Julia, too; most unlike her, such a placid creature normally and they were such close friends. But then I don't suppose dear Michael has had such a big do at St Luke's since he's been there and I know how she worries about him. Of course, it may have been a drop too much of that excellent champagne. Mind you, I had several glasses of it so I may be mistaken.'

Barry was not deceived, he was of the impression Mrs Richardson was rarely mistaken about anything.

'So,' Ian recapped when Barry finished, 'Clayton obviously knew Mrs Henderson rather better than he led us to believe, and he'd been to her house, which he continues to deny.'

'Well his fingerprints told us that much already, and don't forget, when I first spoke to him I said he was holding something back, and on top of that we know he was desperate to see her on Sunday.' Barry ticked off the list of circumstantial evidence on his fingers.

'I know,' Ian interrupted, 'and you're going to mention the reason he had to leave his teaching post, but none of this proves he killed her.'

'You don't think so? Looks like a certainty to me.'

'No. Clayton admitted he knocked on Mrs Henderson's door on that Sunday afternoon but got no reply. It was no secret. He told his wife he was going to invite her over for a drink. She said he was gone only a few minutes and by then she'd been dead quite a few hours. Yes, and you might argue he knew that and only went to make it look as if he didn't. Perhaps he's more devious than I give him credit for, but I don't think so. Now, what you are not aware of is that Bart Henderson, or someone who looks very much like him, was seen leaving her house about nine thirty on Sunday morning. Now if Mrs Richardson overheard correctly the deceased was expecting a visitor on Sunday and didn't want any other callers. Perhaps that someone was her husband and they had serious things to discuss, so serious that he couldn't wait. Instead, while his hosts were sound asleep he drove over and killed her but had to return in the morning to remove some vital piece of evidence. If you recall he refused point blank to go for a walk with them.'

'You think, then, that after a heavy night in the pub—and we've evidence enough to bear that out—he went to bed, got up again in order to commit a murder, drove back and pretended to be asleep when his coffee was brought to him, waited until his friends went out, drove back to Rickenham a second time for whatever reason and returned before his chums got back with the dog. Bit hectic, wasn't it? And if you ask me, a damned sight too cold-blooded. If it was the husband, more likely to be spur of the moment.'

'Put like that, I agree. But he was there.' Without realizing it, Ian was taking his son's side. Mark had only said he thought it was the same man. 'It's on record how much drink that man can hold, probably a lot more than his friends. But the three main ingredients are there: motive, method and opportunity. The motive being jealousy or love. As Judy said, if he couldn't have her nor would anyone else.' Barry sighed. The last thing he wanted to hear were Judy's theories on the case. 'Opportunity I've just explained, and method, well, we know a heavy instrument was used and we know it hasn't been found. And, according to Tom Prendergast and my...another source, there is a piece of furniture which should be in that house and isn't, and that piece of furniture was provided by Bart Henderson. It all fits. What do you say to that?'

'I say we leave it to forensics, they'll know by tomorrow what those pieces were that they found in her skull.'

Each was convinced the other was wrong, but they were not equally convinced their own theories were right. They were using the facts and fitting them to the suspect, a very dangerous game to play. And there was something teasing the back of the Chief's brain, something he was trying to remember. If only he knew what it was.

DETECTIVE CHIEF INSPECTOR Roper and Detective Sergeant Swan interviewed Bart Henderson together, with a police stenographer present. Neither had previously met the man and they were surprised how well he came across, suspecting he'd laid off the juice the night before in order to do so. They were wrong. Bart consumed his usual amount, he was one of those men who, after a night's sleep, or at least, a couple of hours', and a steaming hot shower, appeared none the worse for wear.

'Now Mr Henderson,' Ian said, getting to the point as soon as they were all seated, 'we would like to know why you didn't tell us you were at your wife's house on Sunday morning? Considering the time of her death it seems there is only one possible reason, wouldn't you say?'

'Ex-wife, Chief Inspector. And I should think the answer is obvious.' He was not prepared for this and could not decide if Henderson was being sarcastic or trying to hide his fear. None of the signs were there, the fidgeting or leg crossing, neither were there any visible beads of sweat along his upper lip. Very cool indeed. Unless he was innocent.

'Nothing is obvious to me. Please elucidate.'

'What I told you was true. I was with John and Alice Henley over the weekend and on Saturday night we went to the pub and stayed until closing time. I'm sure you've already substantiated that. But I woke very early, I don't sleep much these days, and I was thinking about Julia and how close I was to Rickenham and I wanted to see her. I spoke to her on the phone on Friday and she said she was busy on Saturday but I could take a chance on Sunday. She didn't promise she'd be in and I knew from her voice she didn't really want to see me and I was undecided whether to take that chance or not. When John and Alice took

Sam out—that's the dog—I made up my mind to come here. I knew it was too early for Julia to be out and I'd be sure to see her, if only for a few minutes. You can have no conception of how much I missed her all the time we were apart and it might seem ridiculous to you but I lived with the hope I could get her back. I know she married me on the rebound but I didn't mind that, I loved her so much I thought it would be enough. I still love her.' There was no hint of sarcasm now. This was no act, only a fool could fail to see his genuine pain and Ian Roper was no fool. He waited without speaking until Bart Henderson was ready to continue. 'I mentioned it to John and Alice on Saturday, that I might pop over and see Julia. From the time she left they've tried to persuade me to put her out of my mind, forget her. As if I could. Naturally they tried to discourage me, Alice said it was time to put the past behind me and make a new life.' He almost spat the next words. 'As if I could without Julia.' Ian was beginning to understand the depth of the man's feelings. Unfortunately for Bart they made the case against him worse.

'So you came anyway, but without telling the Henleys?'

'Yes. They brought me a cup of coffee and said it would do me good to have a long walk in the woods with them and the dog but I refused. By then I'd decided to risk coming. Once they left I drove over. It's not that far, took me about twenty minutes.' Ian already knew that. He had sent a patrolman to do the journey. One way at normal speed, the other way faster like a man in a hurry.

'It's stupid really, a man of my age deceiving my friends over something like that but I couldn't face another of Alice's lectures, nor did I want their pity. And what I feel for Julia is my business. I don't particularly like discussing it with people.

'Well I got here and hung around for a few minutes, sat in the car and stared at the house. The curtains were drawn and it crossed my mind she might have someone in there with her. Then I thought what the hell and knocked on the door. It must have been a good wedding because I couldn't wake her.'

'Excuse me, you said you spoke to her on the telephone on Friday and she told you she was busy on Saturday. Is that correct?'

Bart looked confused. 'Yes,' he answered uncertainly.

'So when did she tell you she was going to a wedding?'

'I don't know. What difference does it make? Last time I saw her I suppose.'

'When you took her the lamp?'

Bart's head jerked back. Good God, they had been investigating his movements. 'It might have been on that occasion, I'm not sure. That was the last time I saw her.' He was not going to give them the satisfaction of asking how they knew.

'We were led to believe Mrs Henderson was expecting a visitor on Sunday. She mentioned it to another guest at the wedding, yet you say the arrangement wasn't definite.'

'No, it wasn't. Perhaps she did really want to see me then.' Ian saw by the glimmer of hope in his eyes that he would live with that thought for a long time to come.

'Chief Inspector, can I ask you something?' Ian nodded his assent. 'Will I be able to attend the inquest?'

'Yes, of course.' He felt a twinge of guilt as he was thanked, for not only would he be able to, his presence would probably be compulsory.

'Whatever you may think I didn't kill her.' Bart saw the coldness in the eyes of his interrogators. 'You do think so, don't you?' He stood, fists clenched but under control at his sides, his voice rose in anger. 'Are you so bloody stupid? How the hell could you imagine for one moment that I could hurt that woman? I loved her. Can't you get that through your thick heads?' Ian and Barry remained calmly in their seats, their suspect was nearer to tears than violence. But was it possible his love had taken him over the edge?

'We'll leave you for a minute or two, Mr Henderson. Sergeant Swan will arrange for a cup of coffee. Or would you prefer tea?'

'Either,' Bart growled as he sat down again, all the fight gone out of him.

Ian had decided it was politic to leave him alone for a while, long enough for him to regain his composure, because he was to be put through something far more harrowing later.

Barry used the break to have a cigarette. When they returned to the interview room Bart was looking less tense.

'I apologize for that outburst,' he said, 'I just can't take it in yet. There's one small consolation though;

if Julia was killed sometime during the early hours of Sunday morning she was still my wife.'

'Technically that's correct,' Ian told him, 'and I take it you are aware you're the sole beneficiary of her will?'

'My God,' Bart said, shocked beyond belief, 'you bastard.'

BART STUMBLED out of the car when it stopped in front of 2 Churchill Way. He was not sure if he could face this, entering her house, a house that meant so much to her, without breaking down completely. But he had to do it. He was not sure if the police had the power to force him but it would appear he was afraid to return to the scene of the crime if he refused.

'Please,' he prayed silently as Barry opened the front door with the key in his possession, 'don't let there be any bloodstains.' But of course there were.

Bart sat in one of Julia's oatmeal-tweed-covered armchairs and tried to avoid looking at the marks on the carpet. He used every ounce of willpower but was unable to control the tears which filled his eyes as he thought of what she must have gone through. Let these bastards think what they like, his loss was real, finally brought home to him by being in the place where she lived, the place in which she chose to live because she could no longer share his home. The place where she died.

'Right,' Ian said, not wanting to give him a chance to compose himself. 'The lamp. Where is it?'

Bart glanced around, unseeing. When he gave it to her she was so much alive. On that occasion she was pleased to see him, only as a friend it was true, but her gratitude was enough to build some hope on. He used her words when he handed her the parcel, 'In friendship, as something to remember our marriage by. Everything in this house has been chosen by you and I'd like you to have this one last thing, the last thing I'll be able to give you as your husband.' Julia accepted the present in the spirit in which it was offered. She was very fond of Bart—horrible word though she thought it—in the way one was fond of a kind, older brother. There were many times when she wished she could offer him more than that friendship.

'She put it there.' Bart indicated a low table in the bay of a corner window. 'Exactly where I imagined she would.' He spoke quietly, remembering how well he knew her, how much better than she knew him.

'It's not here now, we've searched. Can you describe it for us?'

'It was about so big,' Bart held his hand out flat, about three feet from the ground, 'very plain. Julia liked plain things, a sort of beigey colour. It was heavy based so it couldn't be knocked over easily. I bought it from a local man in Saxborough. He makes them. I knew as soon as I saw it that Julia would like it and it matched her colour scheme. The shade was cream silk.'

'And where is it now, Mr Henderson?'

'I don't know. I have no idea. Maybe she changed her mind, decided she didn't want a reminder of me around after all.' Before the Chief spoke Bart realized the implications of the question.

'You see, we have reason to believe it was used as the murder weapon.' Once they were aware of its existence the house and garden had been thoroughly searched and, of course, it explained what the minute particles buried in Julia's scalp were. But surely Henderson hadn't risked carrying it away with him.

'Do you know when the dustbins are emptied in this street?' Barry asked.

Bart's expression was blank. He shook his head, then bowed it. He was defeated. 'It all fits doesn't it? You've got it all sewn up. I cold-bloodedly bring my wife a present, taking the precaution of delivering her means of death a week or two in advance, then come back later and kill her. I'm even seen here at roughly the right time, after I've disposed of the so-called weapon in the dustbin, presumably. And, as you've now told me, I benefit from her will. So, go on then,' he held out his wrists in mock supplication, 'arrest me.'

'We are not placing you under arrest, sir, but we are asking you not to leave your present address unless you tell us your whereabouts. I think that's everything for now. We'll give you a lift back to the station then you're free to go. We'll be in touch.'

They walked towards the door, Bart taking one last look around the room which Julia made so comfortable, but now it seemed empty without the warmth of her presence.

The journey back to the town centre was silent. Bart took his leave with barely a word. 'The dustmen do Bradley Court on a Monday,' Barry said when they were back in the incident room. 'It seems the most likely explanation that the murderer knew that and dumped it, taking a chance that the body would not be discovered immediately. But why dump it anyway? If there were no fingerprints it would have made no difference. Anyone who knew Mrs Henderson would be aware she had no regular habits, that she was unlikely to be missed for a while.'

Ian sighed. 'We'd better get the rubbish dump turned over then, you get on to it will you Barry?' It was likely to be a waste of time and effort, by now the lamp, assuming that's where it was, would be smashed to pieces. Still, forensics might come up with something.

LAURA AND GRAHAM Sutcliffe attended church as usual on Sunday morning, then followed the weekly ritual of drinks with the Morleys at Northfield Farm. Neither of the couples were in the best of moods.

Graham and Laura were still suffering from the indignity and humiliation of their interview with Barry Swan and they had not yet forgiven each other for the blinding row which followed on their return home. On entering the house Graham had reached for the whisky decanter, which prompted his wife to accuse him of becoming an alcoholic 'on top of everything else'. Only then did he round on her and pour out all the pent-up frustrations accumulated during the course of their married life, stunning her into shocked silence.

'Julia wasn't the only one,' he admitted, no longer caring if he went too far, 'there have been one or two others over the years. What do you think it's been like for me, not being able to make love to my own wife? You've always had a wonderful ability to make me feel worthless, in bed and out of it. I'm fully aware you only stay with me for the money, but if you'd ever just shown me one bit of kindness or understanding, ac-

cepted my advances once in a while, I would not have
had to resort to other women.'

Laura had turned her back to him, not wishing him
to witness the tears which threatened. She had had no
idea he still cared for her.

'Laura?' he asked, 'has there ever been anyone else
for you?' The look of contempt she threw him gave
him the answer. He was extremely surprised at the relief he felt.

They had slept in separate rooms but by Sunday
morning were more or less back on an even keel. They
agreed to go to church although they didn't feel up to
it, as their non-attendance would give the town more
cause for gossip. It would be common knowledge by
now that they had been questioned; Mrs Bedlow
would have seen to that.

The Morleys had less reason to be subdued. They
were displeased only because the police had been to the
farm on several occasions now. To see them and to
speak to Gerry Clayton. Their annoyance was due to
intolerance and snobbishness. It did not seem to matter that Julia was dead, brutally murdered, but it was
bad form to have uniformed constabulary and plain
clothes officers tramping all over their land, and why
such people could imagine the killing had anything to
do with anyone they knew was beyond their compre-
hension. And from what Sheila Richardson said when
she telephoned on Sunday evening, it seemed she, too,
had been questioned. 'But then,' Caroline thought,
'she probably enjoyed it, she's so damned public spir-
ited.'

Dennis did the rounds with the drinks, Graham
surprising him by asking for a small one. He was re-

warded with a tight smile from Laura. They sat on the terrace surveying the landscaped garden and the fields beyond. The silence was not important: they had been friends for many years. Yet there was an unspoken feeling that Julia's death had come between them; they felt less free to be open with each other. Dennis was restricted from telling his endless supply of blue jokes about 'other women' now he was certain Graham's indiscretion was known to Laura. At the back of his mind he was aware of a tinge of doubt as to the innocence of his friends. Laura or Graham might have had a motive to kill Julia. But when he thought about it, what lay heaviest was his own guilt. With the exception of Graham they had treated Julia like a leper. They all knew this and they also knew, despite their individual opinions of her, she did not deserve to die.

'When's the funeral to be?' Caroline asked during lunch, the topic never far from their minds.

'No idea,' Graham replied, sure that the question was addressed more to him than anyone else. 'But I believe there's to be an inquest tomorrow. Sometime towards the end of the week I should imagine. Were you thinking of going?'

There was an embarrassed silence before Caroline, with some determination, said 'I think, under the circumstances, we should all go.' Then more quietly, 'It's the least we can do now.' Laura wondered if the comments were made out of genuine regret or with the realization that it would not do any harm to be seen publicly paying her respects.

BART DROVE SLOWLY back to Saxborough. On Friday morning, when he woke and realized Julia was really dead, he was too upset to turn up for work at the university, so he telephoned his apologies, saying he was unwell. There seemed little point to life if Julia was not a part of it, in however small a way. But, unusually, he did not feel the need to drown his sorrows in drink. He spent most of the day in his room, wallowing in nostalgia. In the evening he drank fewer gin and tonics, it was as if he wanted to experience fully the worst thing imaginable, not blot it out of his memory. What he felt when Julia left was nothing compared with his sorrow now. He should not have lied to the police but he stupidly believed they would have caught the murderer almost at once. Instead he had made himself their prime suspect.

There was nothing and no one waiting for him in his lodgings and the thought of interrupting Mrs Roomes from her Sunday afternoon television for the sake of someone to talk to was too much to bear. When he arrived at the outskirts of Saxborough he turned left at the junction of Westgate Street, the opposite direction to that in which he lived, and followed the line of the old city walls until he came to the university. The campus was more or less deserted, few students used the main buildings on Sundays. He would use the time to catch up on grading the essays handed in the previous week. He was a good tutor and gained pleasure in seeing his student do well. He would not let them down.

He parked in the near empty carpark and strolled along to his own office, surprised, as he was in the process of opening the door to see the Principal heading down the corridor towards him.

'Ah, Bart, old chap, there you are.' Julian Wickes addressed all and sundry as old chap, whatever their age or station in life. 'Doing a spot of overtime?' Bart nodded, he didn't want to have to speak, to say words he could hardly bear to think; they would choke him. Under the outward appearance of Old Boy bonhomie the Principal was no fool. One look at Bart's face told him something was seriously wrong. He hoped and prayed his rumoured drinking had not got him into trouble; he would hate to lose one of his best tutors.

'Got a minute?'

'Sorry?'

'Come on, in here, old chap.' Julian Wickes held open the door of the office and waited until Bart was inside before shutting it firmly behind him. 'Got any coffee?' Bart waved towards the top drawer of a filing cabinet where he kept his tea and coffee making apparatus then sat, head in hands, while his superior made them both a drink. When a steaming mug of coffee was placed before him he looked up. His eyes were red-rimmed and dark shadows smudged the sockets. Julian thought if he had been drinking it must have been one hell of a bender.

'Still not feeling too good?' Julian asked, aware of his absence on Friday.

'I wasn't really ill. I'm sorry, I . . .'

'Here, take it easy, old chap.' Bart held out a hand to accept the paper handkerchief he was offered.

'Sorry. Whatever must you think of me?' There was nothing but compassion in his companion's face. 'My wife has been murdered. And the police think I did it.'

'Jesus Christ.' So that was why young Penny was dragged out on Thursday night. Julian was attending a dinner in Colchester but had given telephonic permission for Penny to allow the police to get Bart's file from personnel. This was far more serious than the pub brawl he imagined. But he had known Bart for eleven years, he was not capable of doing such a thing. And poor Julia. He remembered her well, a truly beautiful woman. He also remembered the circumstances of their meeting. Not long after the tragic death of her first husband he and Bart had attended a function at an hotel in London. It was there they met Julia who had been dragged along unwillingly by a friend. After that she came to Saxborough a few times and the next thing he knew she and Bart were married. That was about seven years ago. He suspected it was too soon after her loss for Julia to be thinking rationally; it was no surprise to Julian to hear it hadn't worked out. But knowing Bart, with his bearish good looks, his charm and his eternal optimism, she probably hadn't stood a chance, he would have swept her off her feet. Of course, he was also reliable, intelligent and patient, the very qualities she would have needed at the time. The sad thing was Bart was not prepared to wait, he was so much in love with her he thought it would become infectious.

Julian toyed with the idea of having a word with the police himself to see if he could put in a good word for Bart, along the lines of a character reference maybe. It probably wouldn't do any good; he knew himself that, given the right circumstances, anyone could become a murderer. But not Bart. Surely not he. For the time being he would stay and offer what comfort he could.

'Ah, I'll be back in a sec,' he said as he went off to fetch the bottle of Teachers and two glasses which he kept in his own filing cabinet for emergencies.

EIGHT

ON MONDAY MORNING Moira was spared the usual grumbles and delaying tactics which were part of Mark's ritual as he got himself ready for school. He was in a happy mood. He quite liked school, but he enjoyed bed more. Today, though, he was anticipating with excitement his appointment with his father at the police station. Moira crossed her fingers and hoped nothing would crop up to take Ian out of the office before Mark arrived.

Nothing did. Ian spent a frustrating morning going over the files and cross-checking statements. There were no discrepancies. They were also doing a fuller check on Bart Henderson and were waiting for a reply from the Criminal Records Office. There was still not enough evidence to prove either himself or Barry Swan right. Later, when he was satisfied he had missed nothing amongst the mounds of paper-work in front of him he meant to see Gerry Clayton to ask him what he and Mrs Henderson were arguing about and at the same time see if he could get him to explain how his fingerprints happened to be in the house. 'Odd that,' Ian thought as his eyes scanned a sheet of computer printout, 'if he was so meticulous enough to wipe the lounge clear of prints, why was he so careless elsewhere?' It was possible he wore gloves and took them off too soon, but it also meant that although entry must have been via the back door, unless Julia let him in, he left by the front, not what one would expect. This theory didn't have the ring of probability, didn't give him that feeling in the base of the spine which he experienced when he knew he was right. He was still not convinced the murder was premeditated, it was somehow too brutal. No, a killer would come armed with a knife or a gun, or, if he was strong enough, use bare hands. This had to be done in the heat of the moment. But at six a.m. or thereabouts? It seemed an odd time of day for passions to be so aroused.

The computer print-out back in its folder, Ian doodled idly on a pad. He had to attend the inquest shortly but eyeing what he'd drawn thought he would pay a call at the vicarage. On the paper he'd drawn several crosses.

He wrote himself a few notes, one to see if Brian Lord would have a chat with both Clayton and Henderson, not a request he really liked having to make but knowing his prejudice was not as strong as it once was. Picking up a raincoat, a habit which died hard during this period of the year when the weather was so uncertain, the Chief headed for the door.

'Sir?' Ian turned back. PC Blakelock was holding the telephone receiver towards him. 'Call for you, asked for you especially, a Mr Julian Wickes.' He shrugged and took the phone. The name meant nothing.

NOT LONG AFTER TEN THIRTY, when Laura had been to the off licence to buy her weekly supply of cigarettes and settle up the previous month's liquor bill, she thought she ought to go and pay her condolences to Susan Barfoot. There had been no opportunity after church yesterday because Susan had been surrounded by people doing likewise. It was several weeks since they had been to the vicarage for drinks and she hoped neither she nor Graham had offended the Barfoots in any way. Her motives were not entirely altruistic, she also hoped to hear what Gerry Clayton and Julia were arguing about and any other bits of gossip Susan was likely to be in possession of. It was not so much a desire to hear this gossip but rather to discover if Graham and herself were included in it.

Susan was not pleased to see her.

'Are you terribly busy?' Laura inquired as she stepped across the threshold and made her way towards the kitchen where, she was sure, Susan would have a pot of coffee on the go. And Susan, the perfect hostess, was too polite to say yes, she was busy, that she was about to give the kitchen floor a coat of polish. 'Nothing that can't wait,' she said instead. 'Coffee?'

'Love one.' Susan frowned as Laura lit a cigarette. Laura was a messy smoker, always managing to spill ash down her clothes and scatter it across table tops, and the aroma of the smoke as she blew it out made Susan want one herself. She disappointed her guest by spooning instant coffee into the cups, knowing this would hasten her departure.

'Here you are,' she said, placing Laura's cup in front of her and biting her tongue as she noticed ash already speckling the wood table.

'Thanks. I can't stay long, I just came to say how sorry I am, and Graham of course, about Julia's death. I know how close you were. It's simply dreadful, and to think there's a murderer in our midst.

There are so many sick people around nowadays it seems. Once, something like this would make news headlines, now murders seem to be two a penny and I...' she saw Susan's face.

'Susan, I'm sorry. How tactless of me rambling on like this. You're obviously very upset and all I'm doing is making it worse. Everybody's upset of course, and the police won't let us alone. They have this crazy idea it was one of the guests at the wedding.'

'I know, they've been here too. They knew I knew Julia better than anybody. But I wish they'd stop asking questions, it's bad enough she's dead without that. I wish I could be left alone.'

Laura was too thick-skinned to take the hint. 'Yes, it's a shame. Have you been able to help them? The police? I thought maybe *you* might have some idea who did it.' Susan gripped the edge of the table, her knuckles white. Why did Laura say that? What on earth did she know to make her say it?

It had come out badly, but Laura did not know how else to ask if anyone thought either she or Graham was involved.

'Well, chin up, Susan. If there's anything I can do, you know. Why don't you and Michael come over to us on Sunday? We've been here so often, it'd make a change for you.'

'I don't think so, it's difficult with the boys.' Laura saw it for the excuse it was. The boys were old enough to look after themselves during the day and were always out somewhere when she and Graham were invited round.

As she backed her mini out of the drive she saw, in her rearview mirror, the distinctive form of the Chief

Inspector's car. She braked and waited. Ian nodded an acknowledgement and motioned for her to continue her manoeuvre. It was not her with whom he had business.

Susan had far more difficulty in biting back the retort she would have liked to have made when, for a second time in less than half an hour, she was asked if she was busy. 'No, come in,' she said, looking, to Ian, even more fragile and defeated than she had before.

'Would you like some coffee?' There was no mistaking the resignation in her voice.

'No, I've just had one, thanks.' She showed him into the living-room, leaving him briefly to get a glass of water. 'Are you sure you don't want something?' she asked again, vicarage manners returning.

Ian shook his head, beginning to feel like a regular visitor at the Barfoot's house. 'What can you tell me about Bart Henderson?' he wanted to know when she returned, the Valium starting to work, at least psychologically.

'Bart? Nothing, I've never met him.'

'But you knew of him. Mrs Henderson obviously mentioned him from time to time during your conversations.'

'No, not very often. Julia told me their marriage didn't work out—she took all the blame for that herself, you know, but I don't think anything can be that one-sided—and that he's a tutor at Saxborough University. Other than that she didn't seem to want to talk about him. Michael and I were at Saxborough, but in case you were wondering, it was before Bart's time.'

'And you're quite certain you've never seen him?'

'Positive, Chief Inspector. I wouldn't forget something like that. In fact, I've never even seen a picture of him. Looking at it that way I suppose it's possible he's walked past me in the street somewhere, but I wouldn't recognize him.' This seemed to ring true. The only picture in Julia's possession was the framed wedding photograph found hidden, or if not hidden, pushed out of sight under some papers.

'I see, but I find it rather,' Ian searched for the appropriate word, 'unusual, that Mrs Henderson kept to herself the fact that she and her husband were still on friendly terms and that he went to her home, if not frequently, then at least several times a year. Don't you? I mean considering the closeness of your relationship with her?'

'I had no idea. You must be mistaken, Julia would've told me.' There were two bright spots of colour in Susan's face and maybe, Ian suspected, a shade too much indignation in her denial.

'We have it on his own admission, apart from a couple of witnesses who confirm it.'

'Once again, Chief Inspector, I'm afraid I can't be of any help. Unfortunately your visits here don't seem to be very productive.'

There was nothing more to say. Mrs Barfoot was extremely hard to get through to and Ian felt the interview was over. Susan made sure it was by opening the door and saying 'I really am jolly busy, so if there's nothing else . . .'

'No. Goodbye, Mrs Barfoot.'

Ian turned the ignition key and eased in the clutch feeling very much as if he had been dismissed, but two things struck him about their brief conversation. One was her use of what he thought of as 'School Friend' vocabulary and the other was that although everything she said was plausible, she was lying.

THE INQUEST, as such affairs go, was well attended. Apart from the personnel who had to be there, many townspeople turned up out of idle curiosity. Ian and Barry and PCs Jackson and Stone, who had found the body, sat in the front row. John Cotton, the SOC officer, slouched against the back of an uncomfortable wooden bench, wistfully clutching a packet of cigarettes which he knew he would not be able to smoke until it was over. Bad news for a sixty-a-day man. Bart walked in at the last minute, unaccompanied, and interestingly, placed himself beside Michael Barfoot. Neither he nor his wife showed any signs of recognition.

Individually they were called to give evidence but to Ian, at this stage, the outcome was a foregone conclusion. Doc Harris, who loved his work as a police surgeon, the parts, that is, which did not include the necessity of his presence in a courtroom, reeled off the contents of the post mortem results and answered one or two specialist questions. Next it was Ian's turn. He was not in a position to name the suspects publicly but was able to satisfy the coroner that investigations were well under way. The coroner, for his part, could do no more than ask if there were any objections to his issuing a burial notice. There were none. He passed a verdict of murder by person or persons unknown.

The subdued group finally filed out of the dingy room, the Chief waiting until last to watch Bart Henderson and Michael and Susan Barfoot, waiting to see if they made any sort of contact. Apart from a mumbled 'sorry' when the two men reached the door at the same time, there was no other communication.

Bart stood outside in the watery sunshine which managed not to penetrate the grimed windows of the coroner's court. 'What exactly does the burial notice mean?' he asked as Ian joined him.

'It simply means the funeral or cremation can go ahead.'

'Ah, I thought so.' He paused. 'Chief Inspector, can I, I mean is it in order under the circumstances, for me to see to things? She doesn't have anyone else.' Ian saw how much it meant to him and felt a twinge of pity; not, he thought, what one should be feeling towards a prime suspect.

'I'll pay for everything, naturally. Myself.' It was not yet clear whether he would benefit from Julia's will if he was charged with her murder but when he spoke next he made it quite clear he did not want her money; if anything came his way he would give it to charity. His job, after all, paid more than enough to sustain his meagre lifestyle. The only thing he wanted was the photograph of her which stood on her bookshelf. It was taken one night before they went off to a dinner. Somehow he felt he captured the spirit of her in that picture, she was so alive, so radiant and she was laughing. Bart did not know that at that time the laughter was masking the pain she still felt from the loss of her husband.

'If only I'd tried harder,' he said, 'persuaded her not to go, she might still be alive.' Even as he spoke he knew he could not have tried harder, no man could, just as he had continued to try to win her back ever since their separation.

The chief was watching Bart, watching him closely, and he felt something give. If asked, he would be unable to explain how he knew, but right then he was sure Bart was innocent. His superiors' view was an entirely different matter and investigations against the man could not be dropped on the basis of Ian's gut feeling, but he suspected an effort would be required to put his whole heart into it.

'If you're prepared to pay, I can't see why there should be any objections,' Ian said, 'and I'm sure Michael Barfoot would be only too pleased to conduct the service, Mrs Henderson being such a close friend of his wife.'

'Yes, I'd like that, I'll have a word with him.' Bart did not ask who Michael Barfoot was, so if he did not know the Reverend personally he was at least aware of his existence.

'It's a shame you've just missed him, he was at the inquest.'

'I didn't realize. Julia talked of him and his wife, Susan, quite a lot but I never got to meet them. I didn't particularly want to meet them either. Every minute I had with Julia was precious, I didn't want to share my time with her with others.'

This was something to think upon. Mrs Henderson apparently discussed her life and her friends freely with the man she was in the process of divorcing but did not extend the same confidences to her best and only friend. Ian found that hard to swallow.

The two men parted, Bart to return to Saxborough having once again given his assurance he would be contactable either at his home address or the university, the Chief to the station to telephone Brian Lord. It crossed his mind during the inquest that he would like to be present when Lord interviewed Clayton and Henderson but was not sure if it was allowed. He hoped Lord would agree with his opinion that the latter was innocent. Unfortunately, if this was the case, he would have to listen to Barry Swan's gloating for weeks to come. Unless they were both mistaken.

Surprisingly Ian did not forget Mark was coming to see him after school and he was there to meet him when he arrived. He sent someone to fetch the boy a drink and some biscuits and when he'd eaten them started to show him around. Since his last visit, which was to the old station house, modern technology had rapidly taken over and Mark itched to have a go on one of the computer terminals but was forbidden because of the confidential information they held. He was allowed a peep into the incident room before Ian took him to the busy front office and sat him down with a bookful of photographs and a handful of loose ones which included one of Bart Henderson. It was the original wedding photograph, but to avoid influencing anyone who might be shown, the side where Julia stood had been cut off. In no time at all Mark picked it out.

'That's him, Dad, the man I saw at Mrs Henderson's house,' he said excitedly. Ian ruffled his hair.

'Good lad, that's great. Thanks a lot.'

'Are you going to arrest him?'

'No, not just yet. We don't want to make any mistakes, do we?'

Mark was disappointed. He had hoped his identification would prove to be the solution to the crime but before they were able to discuss it further Ian was called to the phone. He left Mark in the care of Sergeant William Baker and hurried away to the front desk to where he'd been summoned. In front of it stood Gerry Clayton, pale and trembling.

He had come, he said, to confess to the murder of Julia Henderson.

ON SATURDAY AFTERNOON Ann Clayton returned from her shopping trip feeling happy and rejuvenated. She looked better than she had for years. She had been persuaded to go for a russet colour rather than red for her hair and was pleased she took the advice. It emphasized her creamy complexion and the greenness of her eyes and the dress she chose flattered her figure. She had not noticed the pounds drop off since their move from London but was pleasantly surprised to find she could wear a size ten instead of her usual twelve. She parked the car and opened her front door with a feeling of elation and hope for the future. Gerry's reaction hit her like a bucket of cold water.

He was hunched in an armchair in front of the unlit gas fire and the room was chilly. His earlier mood of boredom and frustration had degenerated into one of depression and self-pity. As Ann entered he turned round slowly and let his eyes travel the length of her body.

'We can afford all this, I suppose, on my enormous salary.' It was unlike him to be sarcastic.

Ann's heart sank. With one sentence he had reduced her mood to match his own. Only rarely did he sink to these depths but when he did she dreaded it.

'I didn't spend much, Gerry. I got the dress in a sale. I thought you'd be pleased.' She was near to tears. 'I only did it for you. Don't you like it?'

'No, I bloody well don't. Not the dress, nor your hair. You looked fine before.'

'I thought, well, I thought you were getting tired of me.'

'And why should you think that? Because I don't screw you much? Is that it? I thought you understood about that. Ah, hang on, it's not that is it? You've got someone else, haven't you? Come on, you can tell me.'

'No, of course I haven't. There's never been anyone else.' Ann was shocked he could think so.

'Liar!' he roared, 'sneaking off to Ipswich, poncing yourself up to meet him the minute my back's turned. No wonder you didn't want me to come with you.'

'Oh, Gerry, you're so wrong.' But it was too late. He was out of the chair and across the room before she could move. She fought not to panic, not to aggravate him further as he put his hands around her throat. Gerry wouldn't hurt her, he'd never laid a finger on her before, but her teeth rattled as he shook her and in the seconds before she passed out she realized he might have been capable of murdering Julia Henderson.

Ann was unconscious for less than a minute but it was long enough for Gerry to feel her body go limp in his grasp. He released her immediately and she slid to the floor. His relief was overwhelming when her eyelids began to flicker.

'Oh my God, Ann, what have I done?' He pulled her gently into a sitting position then lifted her into a chair. 'Have I hurt you? Do you want a doctor? Are you all right? Please say you're all right.' She nodded. Her neck was sore but she was okay, just incapable of speech. This was not the man she'd married, the man she thought she knew so well.

'A drink?' he asked. 'Shall I get you a drink? Or coffee?' Ann nodded again. She didn't care which, but while he fetched it she would have time to pull herself together, to decide what she ought to do. She was not afraid, she might be being foolish, but she suspected he was the more frightened of the two.

Gerry's hands shook as he poured two large glasses of red wine from a bottle he found in one of Ann's shopping bags. It was slightly more expensive than the usual plonk they drank and she had intended having it with their evening meal to celebrate her new image and perhaps help Gerry relax a bit.

'I don't know what to say, Ann, I can only apologize. Not that that will alter things. I just don't know what came over me, it was as if I was watching myself. I never thought I'd hurt you. Please forgive me.' She reached out and touched his head as he knelt at her feet. She realized he was crying. 'Do you think I killed Julia?'

More than anything she wished to be able to say no you didn't, but she couldn't because she didn't know and she would not lie.

'Do you think you did?' was the best she could come up with.

'I don't know, it's possible, isn't it? I mean, after what I did to you anything's possible. You wouldn't have heard me if I got up in the night. My finger-prints are in her house, how can you explain that? I certainly can't.' Ann was not certain whether she believed him but thought it politic to remain silent.

Darkness descended slowly that evening, leaving red gashes across the sky promising better weather the next day. And with a new day there would be a new start. Gerry sat thinking over his actions, forgiving Susan Barfoot her outburst now he knew how easily such things happened. It was after nine before he or Ann moved. They didn't talk, they simply sat holding hands in the darkness wondering what was happening to their lives. Eventually Ann cooked the steaks and prepared a salad but they did not enjoy what should have been a special meal. In bed that night Gerry apologized again and reassured Ann that she did look attractive, both of them knowing he should have done so sooner.

The weekend passed. Sometimes there were long silences and sometimes they talked. Gerry went out only once and returned quickly, clutching two more bottles of wine. He was subdued, troubled not only by what he knew he'd done but also by what he was beginning to believe he might have done. By Monday morning he was convinced he was a murderer.

He left the house early and went up to Northfield Farm to see Dennis Morley. He told him he was sorry but he could no longer continue as manager, he hoped he wasn't letting him down too badly but there was a good reason for his leaving. He cleared out his desk and saw to one or two jobs which required immediate attention. From there he went home. He was not sure whether he was pleased or sorry to find Ann out but he wrote her a long letter and left it propped against the kettle knowing it was the first thing she would head for on her return. Then he walked, he did not know where or for how long. All he knew was at four fifteen he presented himself at the front desk of Rickenham Police Station.

JULIAN WICKES was pleased he took the trouble to telephone the Chief Inspector at Rickenham Green. He sounded a decent enough sort of fellow and he believed him when he said his character reference in Bart Henderson's favour might be of some use. But it didn't seem enough. Tuesday was a quiet day for Julian; there were no meetings and no particular problems on the campus. He decided to drive down to Rickenham and see the Chief in person. Bart was not at work on Monday as he had to attend the inquest but he arrived punctually on Tuesday morning, always reliable, drink or no drink. Julian did not tell him where he was going, fearing he would try to stop him.

'Damn shame,' he thought as he packed papers into a briefcase, 'all that emotion going to waste. Pity he didn't meet someone else.' No, he told himself, Bart was no murderer. He was unaware that another man had already admitted to the crime. Once Julian Wickes made up his mind on a subject it took a lot of persuasion to make him change it. All he had to do now was convince the police.

BRIAN LORD made himself available and came, at Ian's request, to assess Gerry Clayton and hand in a written report. He noticed at once the dark shadows under Gerry's eyes and the way in which his hands shook. He looked on the verge of collapse. Brian's initial impression was that, whether or not the man was a killer, he certainly needed help.

Very cleverly, Brian got him to tell the same story over and over again by asking the same questions in a different format. He learned of the move from London and what occurred to precipitate it, then they talked about his short time in Rickenham. Gerry described the awful scene of Saturday afternoon and how it served to convince him he was guilty.

'Why didn't you come forward sooner?' Brian asked.

'I don't know really. I mean I can't actually remember killing her. But I must have. The fingerprints and everything. And the police; all along they thought it was me but couldn't prove it. Now they can stop worrying.'

An hour later Gerry was left in the care of a PC. He was exhausted, the Chief Inspector and his Sergeant had grilled him for almost two hours. He knew what he said was being recorded and he was pretty sure he was being watched through a two-way mirror. The police thought he was holding back. He wasn't. He had pictured his hands around her soft throat, but caressing, not hurting. Had his desire got the better of him? Had he gone to her house in a sleepwalking trance? It was Ann he felt sorry for. What would this do to her?

'We'll have to hold him,' Ian said as he and Barry waited for Brian Lord. 'See to the usual press release, will you? Ah, Brian, come in. So what do you think?'

'An interesting case,' he commented, lighting up a cigarette before he remembered he too was trying to give up. 'There are periods where he doesn't remember. Not amnesia, nothing like that, more of a mental shutter. They seem to occur when he's done something about which he should be ashamed, a sort of ostrich reaction, not a technical term that, but as if he thinks that by completely forgetting the incident it means it hasn't happened. We all do it from time to time, in Clayton's case it's just a little more exaggerated.' Without being told, he guessed the Chief's, and some other police officers', aversion to shrinks of any description, so he was doing his best not to use the terminology of his profession. In his own way he, too, was prejudiced. It was his opinion that the police were not well versed in psychological jargon and he got the impression they thought every killer to be a blood-crazed psychopath.

'Some sort of mental defence mechanism you mean?' Ian asked, taking Mr Lord and his prejudices completely by surprise.

'Yes. Exactly that. Sometimes it's the only way people can live with what they've done. Or what they think they've done.'

'Yes, I see. But has he done it? We can verify what he said about trying to strangle his wife, but he's known for some time we suspected him. Perhaps he went for her because of the strain he was under, and after all, it was only a few months ago he lost his job. Maybe it was the last straw when she spent money he says they can ill afford.'

This was not the way the conversation was supposed to go. Brian was expecting the Chief to come out with some trite phrase such as 'we've got the bastard' much as, some weeks ago, Ian was expecting a lecture on the poor, misunderstood criminal. They were both learning, and as they did so mutual respect began to grow.

'And there's the argument with Mrs Henderson at the reception. He claims he needed someone to talk to, someone other than his wife who at times is *too* understanding. It could be true. From what I gather he doesn't have any male friends, and he strikes me as the sort who gets on better with females. Some men do. I don't know, I'm no detective, that's your baby, but it doesn't add up. There's no motive, or none that I can see at the moment. And murderers always have one, even if it's obscure and doesn't seem like one to the likes of you and me. But with Clayton? I just don't know.'

Ian was experiencing the same doubts. It didn't add up. But he did not want it to be Bart Henderson who was guilty.

Which reminded him. 'There's another chap I'd like you to meet. The deceased's husband, Bart Henderson. Ex-husband actually, as of a few days ago. He was our main suspect and is not out of the woods yet. He was seen leaving her house, outside it anyway, a couple of hours after she died. And he does have a motive. How busy are you? Could you find the time?'

'Sure. When would you like me to see him?'

Ian thought for a second. Bart left immediately after the inquest, which meant he would only have arrived home an hour or so ago. 'Can we leave it till Thursday? By then Clayton'll either have been charged or released. It'll give us a bit longer to get a better picture. I hope we know one way or another by then. Yes, it can wait.'

Brian consulted his diary. A time was fixed for Thursday afternoon.

'Fine. One more favour. When you do the report on Clayton could you include a few notes, you know, a profile of this type of killer?' His own department was working on a psychological profile, but two could do no harm. Ian did not think they were terribly useful; he thought anyone driven far enough could commit murder. Nevertheless he was beginning to like Brian Lord and, true to his own philosophy, wanted to keep on the right side of him. One day he might be needed.

When Brian left, Ian put a call through to the *Rickenham Herald*. Barry had stayed to hear Lord's opinion and had not got round to doing it. Martyn Bright came on the line.

'Got him, have you?' he asked with obvious pleasure, already forming a suitable alliterative headline.

'Not for certain.'

'Oh, shit. Don't tell me. No names, no details, but someone is helping with your inquiries?'

'You've got it in one. Usual statement, please, Martyn.' Ian rang off, chuckling to himself. There was nothing he enjoyed more than frustrating the press.

The silence in the room was now broken only by the ticking of the clock. He looked at it, surprised to see how late it was. He had forgotten all about Mark. By now he must have gone home, once more disappointed in his father. He went down to the main office, quieter now than earlier, and was very pleased to see his son was still there. He sat at an abandoned desk, listening with open-mouthed interest to what Sergeant Baker was saying. A grandfather several times over, albeit a fairly young one, he was entirely at ease with the younger generation and Ian felt a twinge of envy when he saw how comfortable they were in each other's company.

'Dad, Bill's been telling me about the Deben Lane Murders.'

Bill? Since when had his son started calling adults by their first names?

William Baker, happy with his role in life, unambitious for promotion, was nonetheless an extremely observant man. The fleeting furrow of disapproval which appeared across his Chief's forehead had not gone unnoticed.

'Sorry, sir, it's my fault. I asked him to call me that. Not quite so formal I thought.' And with these words he put a stop to any objections Ian was about to make.

'And how are you enjoying the grisly story?'

'It's terrific, great the way he was caught in the end.' Lovely, Ian thought, a set of horrific murders and his son was lapping it up. He was glad it was before his time in the town, for although three women had been killed in exactly the same spot at monthly intervals, it was many weeks before the murderer was apprehended.

'Come on, Mark, time to go home. Your mother will be worried about you.'

'Oh just let me hear the end. Please, Dad?'

Ian smiled. At least his son was enjoying the visit, he only hoped he wouldn't have nightmares. While Sergeant Baker finished the story Ian went to collect his belongings, then returned for Mark who chatted non-stop all the way home.

TUESDAY CAME AND WENT. It was pretty uneventful.

Mrs Bedlow went off to her job at Longrove Park,

all thoughts of Sunday morning a thing of the past. Laura and Graham went about their business and rubbed along much as they always did, except Graham fancied the relationship between himself and his wife was a little less strained than usual. Laura, in turn, decided if her husband was not to be imprisoned it was time to start making the most of what she had. And the Morleys coped perfectly adequately, despite the resignation of their manager. The paperwork was up to date and if anything cropped up Dennis had plenty of people to call on.

Bart spent the day at the university, using his lunchhour to telephone Michael Barfoot to ask if he was willing to conduct Julia's funeral service. He could not bear the thought of having her body cremated and, as there was apparently no stipulation in her will, Bart made the decision himself. If he was not arrested and convicted, he would consider it an honour to look after her grave.

It was Michael himself who answered the telephone. Bart introduced himself and listened to the words of sympathy and regret, wondering if this Christian attitude would alter if he were charged. Michael promised to ring back when he had been in touch with the police mortuary and made the necessary arrangements. The funeral service was to take place at St Luke's but Bart was disappointed to learn Julia was to be buried in the public cemetery and not the pretty churchyard. But of course, in a town the size of Rickenham, it was bound to be full.

There was little more for Bart to do other than pay the bills as and when they arrived; the rest of the formalities had been taken care of by the police. He had been surprised when Michael offered to put him up for the night if he did not feel like making the journey home afterwards, but turned down the invitation knowing he wouldn't be able to bear hearing them talk of Julia. Bart went back to work, finding it hard to concentrate. Julia and the funeral were too much on his mind.

At the station house statements and notes were still being double and treble checked. Each wedding guest had now been accounted for, and knowing Gerry Clayton was sitting in a cell, some of the checking was half-hearted.

Julian Wickes was shown into Ian's office a little after midday.

'Good morning, Chief Inspector. Thank you so much for seeing me. I know what a busy man you must be and there's probably nothing I can tell you which you don't already know, but I felt I couldn't leave things as they are. Bart Henderson is a good friend of mine and I'll do anything I can to help him. If I'm wasting your time, please tell me, but I felt I had to see you in person.'

'Mr Wickes. Good morning, or afternoon should I say. Please have a seat.' Ian was taken aback at the man's forthright attitude but he was also annoyed with himself. Wickes had mentioned driving down when he telephoned with his strange idea of giving Henderson a character reference as if he were applying for a job rather than suspected of murder. It was too late now, the polite thing was to give him a few minutes before he was sent on his way.

Wickes reiterated what he had already told Ian. He left no stone unturned, speaking openly about Bart's work, his personal life and his drinking.

'Mind you,' he qualified, 'that only started after Julia left him. I don't know if any of this has been useful but I felt it my duty to come and see you, both as his employer and his friend. I just hope I haven't done more harm than good. I wouldn't want you to imagine he killed her in a drunken rage. Drink doesn't take Bart that way, it mellows him, makes him affectionate. And he loved her, Chief Inspector, there's no doubt about that. Oh, one more thing.' Ian sighed. Wickes had already taken up fifteen minutes of his precious time. 'I'd like to attend the funeral. Do you happen to know when it's to take place? I'd rather not ask Bart unless I have to.'

'Sorry, I don't know. Mr Henderson is arranging it himself. But you could contact the Reverend Barfoot at St Luke's, it's just up the road, I think he's officiating. Thank you for your time, Mr Wickes, now if there's . . .'

'No, no. Nothing else. Thank you for listening.' He turned to leave. 'The Reverend Barfoot, did you say?' Ian was struggling to hide his exasperation. Was the man never going to go? He nodded, picking up a memo from his desk, surely a big enough hint. 'Couldn't be the same chap who did so well at Saxborough, could it? Michael Barfoot? He stayed on to do his post. grad. Brilliant student.'

Ian's interest was re-aroused. This was yet another link between the people involved.

'Yes, he was at Saxborough. You remember him?'

'Only too well. Hard worker, only interested in his books. Unusual in the 'sixties with the so-called sexual revolution going on. Most of them were too busy secretly experimenting with pot and their new-found freedom to get much work done. Amazing how many still managed to get their degrees. It shook me when he got married. I thought he'd wait until he'd settled down somewhere and pick a nice, quiet, country girl. Funny little thing, the wife. Can't recall her name now but she stood out in her own way. It struck me as odd that he chose her and I wondered if he had to marry her. Still,' he smiled, 'people can't understand why my wife chose me.' But Ian was beginning to understand. In the short time he knew him he concluded that Julian Wickes was a considerate, caring man, one you'd be glad to have on your side. They said their good-byes but Ian knew he would be seeing him again.

LATER THAT AFTERNOON Brian Lord appeared with a couple of typewritten sheets of paper. 'This may be of some use,' he said, 'it's the best I can do in the time and it's been knocked together. I've got a meeting to attend but I'll have a proper report ready by the morning.'

'Great. Thanks.' At this point anything was better than nothing. With a wave of his hand Brian departed.

Ian sat with his elbow on the desk, chin resting between his thumb and index finger, the pose he adopted when he was thinking hard. Clayton was being held in a cell for twenty-four hours. That time would expire at seven thirty tonight. The way things were going he believed that time would have to be extended for a further twelve hours, then, if Clayton was not charged during that period, they would need a Magistrate to authorize them to hold him for a further sixty hours. If he still wasn't charged he had to be released. So, he calculated, they had until seven thirty on Friday to make a decision. And God help them all if it was the wrong one.

There was nothing to be gained by brooding; he might as well read Brian Lord's report. It was, as he said, not much to go on, merely an outline of a personality capable of beating a victim to death. The report on Clayton himself was to follow later as it would require far more work.

What Ian was reading took into account the lack of immediate sexual motive, this was no rapist afraid of discovery. In Brian's opinion the murder was not committed by a casual passer-by. This corresponded to their own theories. He suggested the person might be suffering from one or more kinds of mental illness, perhaps some form of paranoia, likely to be of the persecutory, delusional type, but more probably the perpetrator suffered a personality disorder. 'A controversial one this, Ian,' Brian had written in neat handwriting in the margin. 'I go along with Schneider here, I don't think a personality disorder is an illness. There's no norm, just a comparison with "the man in the street", whoever he may be. Does Clayton fit the pattern?' The next paragraph was concerned with abnormal jealousy, the irrational emotion often leading those in its grip down the path of drink and drugs, these very agents causing disinhibition which could lead to murder. Here, in the margin, was simply the word 'Henderson?'.

As he read on Ian formed a picture of what they should be looking out for. Unfortunately both suspects fitted the bill. But so did Laura Sutcliffe who was never long out of his thoughts. Cold, calculating, admitting to jealousy, she could not be ruled out. And would a man require so many blows to ensure his victim was dead? Would not a man, in the heat of anger, use his bare hands as Clayton had done on his wife? But there was something else. Some of the pieces of the jigsaw began to fall into place and suddenly Ian knew he was about to solve the case.

'Enough,' he told himself as he handed the report to Judy Robbins who happened to be passing as he left his office. 'Do me a copy of this, love, will you?' She smiled and went to do his bidding although she was just going off duty.

Having extended the time Gerry Clayton could be held for a further twelve hours, Ian went home. He was early for once and was delighted to see one of the best sights in the world when he entered the kitchen to say hello to Moira. On the cooker was a saucepan containing a foil-covered bowl. And he, as a detective, knew it could only mean one thing. There was steak and kidney pudding for dinner.

When the meal was over and Mark had gone upstairs to do his homework Ian picked up the evening paper to see if there was anything on television worth watching. 'There's a play on at nine,' Moira volunteered. 'I wouldn't mind watching it.' He grinned. Moira was not usually assertive, never made demands, but because of her unselfish placidity he could never refuse her.

'We'll settle for that then,' he told her, content to read the paper until it was time for it to start.

Moira disappeared upstairs and he heard her chatting to Mark. When she returned she was carrying two small bottles and some cotton wool. She uncapped one of the bottles and poured a small amount of its contents on to the cotton wool. Ian's head jerked up.

'What's that? What're you doing?'

Moira was startled and dropped the cotton wool. 'My nails,' she said, bending down to retrieve it. 'What did you think I was doing?'

'Yes, but what's in the bottle?'

'Nail varnish remover. Ian what's got into you?' She held it up and peered at the label as if a dangerous substance had come into her possession by mistake.

'I thought so. Acetone. That's what didn't fit. Well, well.'

But he couldn't be sure. Not one hundred per cent certain as he needed to be. For the rest of the evening he was deep in thought. Moira watched the play without interruption, then went to make a cup of tea, kissing him on the forehead as she passed.

'You go on up if you want,' he said, 'I've got a couple of things I want to think about.'

Ian wished it was morning. He wanted to be in his car on his way to see the man he thought could provide the vital clue. Clayton was still sweating it out in the cells. They'd have to make a decision about him soon, but he thought he knew what that decision would be. But in the end no decision was necessary. A telephone call changed everything.

NINE

MICHAEL BARFOOT had a lot on his mind. He had spoken to Bart Henderson about the funeral arrangements, pleased to be asked to perform this one last rite, but so very sad it was necessary. And there was Susan; her behaviour was worrying him. He made full allowance for her grief but she was becoming more and more neurotic and it was affecting the boys, especially Matthew, who had not been to school this week. The GP could find nothing specifically wrong with him and Michael trusted him. Of course, the thrashing he received on Saturday might have something to do with it. He could not get over Susan's treatment of the boy. Neither of them believed in physical punishment and the boys, even when they were small, were good. It had never been necessary. He blamed no one but his son for his actions, explaining why it was wrong to steal, but there had to be more to it than that. As a boy he was stupid enough to do the same and was frog-marched back to the shop to apologize. The acute embarrassment he suffered did far more good than a walloping. But he believed with Matthew, there was more to it than a teenage dare.

On Saturday afternoon he had returned from a christening and Matthew came running down the stairs to meet him, sobbing out the tale of what had happened. To Matthew's dismay his father insisted on inspecting the damage and was horrified to see red welts were still visible. Since then every attempt to speak to Susan met with resistance. She refused to stop whatever she was doing for longer than to say yes or no. It was time to press the issue and get her to see Doctor Southgate. The use of chemicals to mask grief was abhorrent to him but under the circumstances it might be the only way to restore sanity to his household.

Tonight he would make a final effort. If he failed again he would get her to the surgery if it meant dragging her there.

'Blast,' he thought, remembering it was Wednesday, the night Susan went off to her evening classes. But he found it hard to imagine her going in the state she was in.

He was amazed when she said she was going but decided not to try to dissuade her. This might be the start of her recovery; it was a good sign if she felt she could concentrate on something other than the awful events of the past week. Their discussion must wait.

'In fact, Michael, I'm almost looking forward to it,' she told him before she left. 'And there's something I want to discuss with Mary.' Mary was a girl who apparently shared his wife's avid interest in writing and had recently had an article published. It was the longest sentence she had uttered all week.

'You must do whatever you think best. I'm sure it'll do you good to get out,' he said, reaching out to stroke her blonde hair but missing as she ducked quickly past him.

It was six thirty. Susan picked up her car keys, kissed Matthew and Josh and headed for the door. She paused for a moment and looked at her younger son. 'Are you all right, Josh? You're very pale.'

'I've got stomach ache.'

'Michael, could you give him a couple of junior aspirins and make sure he's in bed early. See you later.'

Michael did as he was directed and Josh was tucked up in bed before his normal bedtime. It was around eight when he heard him call out and he went immediately to investigate. Josh was lying on top of the bed, flushed and obviously in pain. A couple of tears ran down his face. This was not down to recent events. The boy was ill.

'Josh. What is it? Are you hurting badly?' The boy nodded, another spasm of pain causing him to draw his legs up to his chest.

'Lie still. I'll get Doctor Southgate. Don't worry, you'll be all right.' He ran down the stairs to telephone, praying he was not wrong.

Within a few minutes of examining him Doctor Southgate called for an ambulance. He was sure it was appendicitis. While they waited Michael looked up the number of the school in Ipswich where Susan attended her classes. He spoke to the secretary, and at first did not take in what she was telling him.

'I'm sorry, sir, we no longer hold a creative writing class here. Maybe it's another school. Adult education classes are held in quite a few round here.'

'No, it's your school, I'm sure. My wife attends every week. Could you check your register for me, you must have a list or a record of the students?'

He gave the woman Susan's full name and their address and waited, certain she had made a mistake.

'No, I've checked everyone alphabetically and there's no one listed under the name of Susan Barfoot. If it's any help we did creative writing classes up until last September but they finished because of lack of interest. Would you like the telephone numbers of the other schools?'

'No, it's all right. Thank you.' There was no time to consider where Susan might or might not be because the ambulance had arrived. One of the men picked Josh up very gently and carried him down the stairs. He looked small and vulnerable wrapped in the red blanket. He couldn't leave Matthew on his own, not in the state he was in, so he told him he must come too.

'They're bound to keep him in overnight, if only for observation,' the driver told Michael, 'do you want to follow in your car? Don't worry, he'll be in good hands,' he added seeing Michael's worried expression.

But they all had to go in the ambulance. Susan had the car.

'Will he have to go to Ipswich?'

'No. Redlands. They still do surgery there. If it's necessary, of course.'

It was a relief to know his son would not be far away, visiting would be so much easier. The drive took ten minutes but to Michael it seemed an age. He made up his mind before they arrived at the hospital what had happened. Susan was simply attending a different school and either forgot to tell him or he hadn't taken it in.

Josh, as a child arriving in an ambulance, took priority, so they only waited a few minutes before a doctor saw him and confirmed the diagnosis. He was to be observed overnight but if his condition worsened they would operate immediately. Michael signed the necessary paperwork and while his son was being made comfortable in bed went to the pay phone and rang the vicarage. There was no reply. Returning to the ward he felt a lump in his throat as he saw Matthew was sitting by the bed holding his brother's hand. They were rarely together now, preferring the company of friends their own ages, but they still got on well. Having been reassured there was nothing more he could do and as Josh was beginning to look sleepy, he decided to let him settle down and go home to wait for Susan. She would be frantic if she returned and found everyone out. Too late now, but he should have left a note.

Only when Matthew was in bed did Michael start to worry in earnest about his wife. She did not usually return until ten thirty or even eleven if she stayed on talking, which was fine when he thought he knew where she was. Now it was not fine. Her son was in hospital and there was no way of getting in touch with her. His stomach muscles tightened with anxiety. His wife was nowhere to be found and Julia's killer was still unapprehended. Had something happened to Susan, too? He waited until ten thirty five then could stand it no longer. He picked up the telephone and dialled the number for Rickenham Green Police.

The desk sergeant took the message and recorded it before ringing the Chief at home, praying they did not have a second murder on their hands. Deep in thought, a freshly-brewed mug of tea in his hand, Ian took the call. So Mrs Barfoot was not at evening classes. He had better investigate.

IAN POPPED UPSTAIRS to tell Moira he had to go out then drove to the station. He placed a call to Julian Wickes stressing it was imperative he spoke to him right away. He was lucky, the man was at home and agreed to do as Ian requested. At eleven forty-five Ian, Barry and a WPC set off for the vicarage. They already knew Mrs Barfoot had returned home unharmed because Michael rang back not long after his initial call to say so. Lights were on in the downstairs rooms and the car was parked on the drive.

'Mrs Susan Barfoot,' Ian said as he stood on the doorstep, 'we are arresting you for the murder of Julia Henderson.' Barry Swan read her her rights and she listened silently, making no objections to the charge.

THE FUNERAL was not postponed but Michael had found a replacement to conduct the ceremony. Even if Bart Henderson had not minded, he was not in a fit state to perform his duty. And the press would have a field day when they learned the husband of the person arrested for the murder had been the one to bury the body. For the sake of the boys he must keep as low a profile as possible. They were his main concern now and he could not begin to guess how this would affect them. There was also the consideration he might be asked to leave the church. These were rational thoughts for a man in his position but he was deep in shock. The police would have to release Susan. She was innocent.

Ian did not attend the funeral. It was originally his intention to see who else turned up and watch their reactions. It was not uncommon for murderers to attend the funerals of their victims. His presence was no longer necessary. He cursed himself for being so stupid. The signs were there, he'd seen them but had been unable to interpret them. One consolation was that he and Barry were both wrong.

The coolness with which Mrs Barfoot accepted everything was unnerving and Ian wondered how her husband had lived in the same house and not realized something was dreadfully wrong. Conversely, of course, his wife was amazing in her capability of retaining a facade of normality. Knowing what he did now, he realized instability was the norm for her. So many lives had been ruined. Bart's, for whom the thought of winning Julia back was his reason for getting up in the morning; Gerry, who would have to live the rest of his life with the stigma of being arrested for murder, even though he was innocent, and what remained of the Barfoot family. Those two poor, innocent children. What torments would they have to suffer at school? Any school. It would not matter where they went, people always found out. He hoped they would survive.

Ian knew they were not, and could not be, his problems. His job was to attend to the paperwork and prepare the case for court and this, of course, was not the only crime he was working on, it was just that more minor cases were pushed to the bottom of the pile temporarily. Once this was over the daily grind of mundane issues would reassert itself. Tension easing its way out of their bones and joints, the officers were content to sit and discuss the events of the previous day for a while, to hear the explanations of how and why everything had fallen into place. Relations were back to normal, that is Detective Chief Inspector Roper no longer addressed his men by their first names nor, for the time being, their rank.

'I CAN'T UNDERSTAND IT. How were you so sure?' Moira asked on Thursday evening as she dished up a casserole. 'When I went to bed last night I didn't think you were any closer to solving it. Next thing I know you're off and Susan Barfoot has been arrested.'

'Well, it's like this,' Ian replied as he picked a slice of crispy brown potato off the top of the casserole, regretting his action immediately as he burned his tongue. 'What clinched it was something you did, something that made my hunch seem viable, but I must admit, it was something I should have taken notice of before.'

'Something *I* did?' Moira was curious. She had not known any of the things she did had criminal implications.

'Um, last night. Pass the salt would you, love?'

'Oh, Ian, I put plenty in it, taste it first.' But she got up to fetch it from the worktop, acknowledging the fact she would never change her husband's eating habits.

'Here. Go easy. So tell me, what did I do?'

'Your nails.' Ian swallowed another steaming forkful, wishing the conversation could wait until he'd eaten this delicious meal.

'My nails!' She stared at him incredulously. There were times when he could still surprise her. 'I remember, you wanted to know what was in the bottle.'

'It was the smell you see.' She waited. Ian was chewing thoughtfully, sorting out in his mind what had been intuition and what was fact. She knew he would tell her eventually, when he could present the case chronologically.

'And there was something else, hardly circumstantial evidence I know, but it came to me on my first visit to Mrs Barfoot. It was a quotation. I can't for the life of me remember which part of the Bible it comes from, my Sunday School days are too far in the past, but it's the one about washing away one's sins. Something like that anyway.'

'Corinthians?' Moira suggested, there was something along those lines there. She sat down to get on with her own meal, amazed at the way in which Ian's mind worked. When it came to the job nothing was irrelevant, not even the Bible.

'She was always cleaning. You were here when Mark said as much, and she took it to the point of obsession. Where is Mark, by the way?'

'Out with a friend, he'll be back soon.'

'Oh. Brian Lord was very helpful too.' Moira smiled, guessing the mutual admiration which was building up between him and the psychologist. 'He gave us an outline of the type of personality we ought to be looking for. But we'd been viewing it from the wrong angle, trying to make the picture fit our suspects instead of searching for someone who might fit the picture. Are you still with me?' Moira nodded. It was understandable why the mistake was made, especially when one of the suspects admitted to the murder.

'Then what Julian Wickes told me confirmed my suspicions.' Ian cast his eyes around the kitchen until he saw what he wanted. He got up to cut a thick slice of bread to mop up the gravy. Moira made no comment. She had to admit she secretly enjoyed cooking for a man who so obviously enjoyed his food and ate whatever was put in front of him.

'He came to see me, he's Henderson's boss and wanted to try to help clear his name. God knows how he thought he could do that. Anyway, he mentioned Susan Barfoot, he remembered her from her university days. At the time Clayton was in custody but I felt I ought to question him further. Even an intelligent man with a good memory does not remember one particular student after all those years unless, as he himself put it, there's something odd or unusual about them. Michael Barfoot he could recall because he was an exceptional student. But to remember his girl-friend? No. There had to be more to it than that. I like Wickes, he seems the kind of man that makes time and effort for his friends. Um.' Ian sat back in his chair, his plate wiped clean. Moira knew what was coming next. 'There isn't any more, is there?'

'Yes, but it's for Mark.'

'Ah well, never mind. Where was I?'

'Julian Wickes.'

'Yes. Wickes. After you'd gone to bed I got a call to say Mrs Barfoot was possibly missing. She wasn't, but her husband was worried about her. It was then, when she wasn't where she was supposed to be, that I got on to Wickes. I thought I knew but I had to make sure. He lives on the campus so it wasn't too much to ask him to go and dig out her file. He was obliging but warned me it might no longer be in existence. However, we were in luck. The file showed she was neu-rotic even then. At one stage she was under regular treatment from the college shrink because she'd de-veloped a compulsion to keep washing her hands.

They were red and raw. Her behaviour was put down
to examination stress, very common among students.
Some go as far as committing suicide. Not long after
that she gave up her course to marry the Reverend and
was no longer their concern. Wickes also mentioned
that had she stayed she would not have made the
grade. She tried hard but just wasn't good enough.'

'I've got all that so far, but what about my nails?
You haven't told me that bit yet.'

'I was coming to it. It was the second time I went to
the vicarage that I smelled the acetone. It was only
faint because she'd been baking, but it was definitely
that. I should have spotted it at once. Mrs Barfoot has
very short, beautifully clean, white nails. Everything
about her is immaculate. And she doesn't wear make-
up. Now someone who doesn't use cosmetics is unlikely to paint her nails, wouldn't you say? And in the
post mortem it was stated that Julia Henderson,
equally well groomed but much more glamorous, had
smudged red polish on the nails of her right hand.
"Crimson Inferno" I think forensics said it was.'

'I think I'm beginning to see.' She was. She realized how important a comparison of the two wom-
en's personalities was when it came to drawing
conclusions. 'So,' she said, 'someone like Susan would
have no need of the remover and someone like Julia
Henderson would never go around with smudged
nails.'

'Exactly.'

'But if I'm reading you right Mrs Henderson must
have been killed before the polish dried. I can't believe she was giving herself a manicure at that time of
day.'

'Well it seems she was. We already knew she kept strange hours. Sometimes she wrote late into the night and on occasions all night, if she was in the mood. And the previous night she didn't get back from the reception until very late; she probably didn't bother to go to bed at all. A neighbour confirmed he saw the glow of a light from her house when he had to get up for the toilet, and that was at three thirty, so presumably she was still awake then. Maybe she was typing and chipped the polish. There was a sheet of paper in the typewriter with the beginning of an article on it, but we can't be sure. Maybe she did her nails every day. We'll never know now.

'The light was not on when we arrived on the scene for the simple reason it was no longer there. It was the one her husband gave her and with which she was killed.'

'But if Susan went to the trouble of destroying or hiding or whatever she did with the lamp, why didn't she throw away whatever it was that got nail polish on it? It doesn't make sense.'

'It does if you know Mrs Barfoot and the way she operates. She could get rid of the evidence because it belonged to someone she hated, but she could not accept the idea of throwing away a perfectly serviceable skirt. She admitted she didn't notice the slight stain at first, the material being white and covered in flowers, but saw it when she went to put it in the washing machine. She even thought about leaving it but became nervous after my second visit. And, more important, money's very tight in that household, they just get by on what the Reverend earns, and only then because of his wife's frugality. She has very few clothes and the disappearance of one of her skirts would not go unnoticed, especially as she made it not long ago, ready for the spring.'

'OK. What did she do with the lamp then?'

'As I thought. No, to be fair, as Barry thought. The dustbins on the estate are emptied on Monday evenings. Mrs Barfoot was aware of that and on her way out, and this will give you a clue how calculating she was, she took off the shade and crushed it, then put it, along with the base, in a bin liner she found in the kitchen and dumped the lot in the dustbin. She did not even bother to wipe off her fingerprints knowing they would already be all over the house. She was very confident the body would not be discovered for a day or two and by that time the murder weapon would be safely buried under tons of rubbish down on the municipal tip.'

'Are you saying she then went home, cooked breakfast for her husband and children and went to church, as if nothing had happened?'

'Yes. She did indeed. But as Michael Barfoot now admits, it was only a matter of time before she came to us. She was getting more and more neurotic. He wanted her to see a doctor. When we searched the house we found the acetone, hidden on a shelf along with a bottle of Valium. She's been taking it for years apparently, and he knew nothing about it.'

'But the classes, where she was supposed to be? What've they got to do with it?' Ian yawned. It had been a very tiring week. 'Come on,' he said, 'I'll give you a hand with the dishes and I'll tell you the rest over a whisky.' At that moment Mark bounced in through the back door and Ian knew he could not discuss it further until he was in bed.

ON THURSDAY MORNING the Chief and Sergeant Swan finished off their reports and while they did so Gerry Clayton telephoned. He was still worried, this time that he might be charged with wasting police time. He did not sound too reassured when Barry said he was in the clear. 'Well, if you're sure,' he said, 'and by the way, I've thought about it and Ann agrees, we're not going to leave Rickenham. I can't keep running away every time something goes wrong.' Dennis Morley was generous enough to offer him his job back although he was to have Wednesday afternoons off to attend a therapy group on Brian Lord's recommendations. It was Brian who solved the question of his fingerprints being in Julia's hallway, although, at the time, the police were sceptical. He had knocked on Julia's door one afternoon when Ann was out, with the same purpose as that of his visit to the vicarage: he wanted to pour out his troubles to someone. Julia had allowed him no further than one step inside the door, misinterpreting his motives. She wanted Ann as a friend and was not going to let Gerry's advances spoil it. Although he begged to be allowed to speak to her she sent him away. He had forgotten the episode. It transpired the argument at the wedding reception had been over the same subject. He'd been desperate for someone to talk to, no more than that, but Julia's experience with men led her to think otherwise. She was angry and told him in no uncertain terms that enough was enough, she was fond of Ann and did not want him visiting her house alone. Only with Brian's gentle expertise had these facts emerged. There was no question of the Chief's ability as a trained interviewer—no one was better at getting the truth out of someone trying to conceal it—but he had failed with Gerry Clayton because the man himself did not know what was the truth. Hopefully the therapy would help.

Barry replaced the receiver in its cradle. 'Have Mrs Barfoot's parents been notified?' he asked.

'There's only her mother now, but yes, she has been. The father died about eighteen months ago and until today, Mrs Barfoot didn't know it.'

'My God, didn't they keep in touch at all?'

'No, it seems not, because Mrs Bentley, the mother, wasn't aware she had any grandchildren.' Ian thought it sad but knew the same thing could happen to him if he continued to ignore his son. It was up to him, while the boy was still young, to make the effort.

SUSAN SAT IN HER CELL, motionless, uncaring. Soon they would come for her and ask her more questions. This time she would tell them everything. They were more intelligent than she gave them credit for. The breakfast they provided lay uneaten on a tray, the coffee, which was instant, she rejected after two or three sips.

They had told her mother, of course, although she hadn't provided the address. She wasn't sure she lived in the same house. And her father was dead. It was difficult to feel any sorrow when she hardly knew him. How had her mother taken the news?

At nine o'clock the door was unlocked and a WPC came to take her to an interview room. She was led up two flights of concrete steps and sat at a table. The

WPC did not speak to her but remained standing just inside the door. Two men entered, the first she knew, the Chief Inspector, the second was Barry Swan. She was asked her full name and noted, as she answered, the recording machine had been switched on. Ian gave the date and the time. She had already said she did not want her solicitor present and was asked to repeat this for the record. Before the interview began she stated, without preamble, 'I killed Julia Henderson. And I have no regrets.'

There was a sharp intake of breath from Barry but he controlled whatever shock he felt.

'Why did you kill her, Mrs Barfoot?' The Chief's tone was gentle.

'Because I hated her.' She was telling the truth and the men present knew it. They could not, however, wrap up the case on her admission. Many people confessed to murders they had not committed. They still needed proof.

'Why did you hate her?' This was going to be hard work. Susan's face was set, hard and uncompromising.

'She took everything from me that I'd worked so hard for.'

'Such as?'

'She wanted Michael. He couldn't see it, but I knew.'

'Your husband. She was having an affair with him?'

'No, but she wanted to. And the children.'

'I don't understand what you mean. You say Mrs Henderson and your husband were not having an affair, yet you claim she took him from you.'

'It was only a matter of time. He'd have given in in the end.' Ian shook his head and remembered Brian Lord's report. Was this what he meant by abnormal jealousy? 'You mentioned your children. Can you elucidate?'

'She was always smarming round them, wanting to see what they'd done in school, asking them in for a drink. She tried to turn them against me. She even let them use their paints on her dining table.' The disgust in her voice was plain, and in keeping with her obsessional cleaning habits. 'As if she didn't have enough already. Two husbands, think of that Chief Inspector, and she wasn't content with that, she wanted mine too. And Gerry Clayton. He was my friend before he knew her. She couldn't bear to see him friendly with me, she wanted him as well. I was going to sleep with him you know.' They didn't know and suspected neither did Gerry. How much of what she said could they believe?

She saw their expressions. 'You think I'm mad, don't you? I'm sure you already know I had some treatment once, but it was years ago, at university. It was only exam nerves. I could have passed if I wasn't so nervous. I worked so hard to get there, to please my parents, they didn't know how difficult it was. They were quite old when they had me and I was the only one. They wanted the best for me. I had lovely clothes you know, and they made sure I didn't mix with anyone rough. I couldn't play out in the street for instance. It wasn't any good though. I was never good enough. I got a B, a C and an E for my 'A' levels and I knew they expected As. Well, it's too late now. I gave it all up to marry Michael. They wouldn't have liked him, he's not rich and successful and he's...but I didn't fail him. Not once. All the time I've been married I've never let the standards drop. And Michael was proud of me, he knew no one else could have done so well. He admired me for the way I kept the house and looked after the children.' She was using the past tense, her subconscious registering the fact they would no longer be together.

'When did you start taking Valium?' Susan met his eyes. So they had searched the house already.

'A long time ago. At university.' They did not press her for the name of the prescriber.

'And your relationships with other men? Your Wednesday nights out? Your husband thought you were attending evening classes, but this has not been the case for the past few months, has it?'

'Is this relevant?'

Barry intervened. 'We believe it is, Mrs Barfoot.'

'I did go to classes for a while. A creative writing group. But it broke up in the end, not enough people were interested. I was going to leave anyway. No one liked me and everyone criticized what I wrote. On one occasion the tutor used something I did as an example of how not to write. I was very upset. After the class one of the men there asked me out for a drink. I went because I didn't want Michael to see me in a state. He was nice, he asked me lots of questions about myself. I thought he was genuinely interested. He was, what's the word? Sympathetic. Yes. I told him how hard I worked, how my whole life was spent cleaning. Oh yes, cleaning and more bloody cleaning, scrubbing away at the dirt. The whole world's full of dirt you know. It's everywhere. It's in the streets and it gets into the house. And there's always dirt in bedrooms. God, the sheets. It's filthy. Sex is filthy. I hate it.' The Chief was noting down all her contradictions.

'You hate it, you say, yet you slept with several different men during the past year?'

'Why do you keep asking? I told you last night that's where I'd been.'

'I'm sorry if I'm missing the point, Mrs Barfoot, but I can't see why, if you didn't like sex, you went out of your way to find it.'

'I couldn't keep up with it. The housework. It was getting me down. Dirt everywhere. Michael was beginning to notice, I saw the way he looked at me sometimes, as if he pitied me. Because I wasn't good enough. Well if there was going to be dirt I might as well contaminate myself as well. That would teach him to expect so much.'

'You were trying to pay your husband back for something you imagined he felt? And you thought having sexual intercourse with other men would do this?'

'Yes. I did. Peter, the first man, from the writing group, said a bit of dirt never hurt anyone. He was so stupid. I asked him what he thought was dirty.'

'What did he say?'

'He said "hurting other people needlessly, child abuse and the taking of a life".'

'If you wanted to make your husband suffer, why keep your actions a secret?'

'I thought he'd find out, that he'd suspect something. He didn't though. That's why I was going to have sex with Gerry. Nearer to home, he'd be sure to find out. He even suspected it was on my mind. Then Julia spoiled it all. The bitch.'

'And that's the only reason you killed her?'

'Yes. She was a filthy bitch. She slept around. Never satisfied. And once I thought she was my friend. And she got worse, wearing those clothes, drawing attention to herself as if to say look at me, look how beautiful I am. The way she behaved she was asking to get killed.'

Ironical, Ian thought. While other women of the town were renowned for holding this view, it was the person who was supposed truly to like her that hated her most.

The Chief decided he had listened to enough self-pity and got the interview back on more practical lines. If Mrs Barfoot was guilty she would be able to answer questions only the killer could know. He began by asking her her exact movements on Saturday night. All she said tied in with other statements given by Michael Barfoot and various wedding guests, up to and including the taxi ride home.

'What was said in the taxi? What was it that Mrs Henderson told you that pushed you over the top?'

'She said Gerry wanted to see her alone, to go to her house and talk to her. As if she didn't have plenty of men eating out of her hand already. And I knew, even though she didn't say, that Bart was creeping around all the time, wanting her back. The thought of it makes me sick.'

'And after that?'

'I went home to bed. But I couldn't sleep, I kept thinking about her and everything she'd got and no one seemed to care that she was a slut. There were times her house was a mess, papers and coffee cups all over the place. A pigsty.'

'And Sunday morning?'

'Michael and the children were sound asleep. I crept out about six fifteen and walked down to Julia's house. I was going to give her a piece of my mind. I guessed she'd probably be up all night, she said she might do some writing. I walked in, the back door was open. And she was sitting there painting her nails, in a satin housecoat just like some Hollywood actress, and she was going to take my husband away. I don't know what happened. I just couldn't bear it. She was sitting in an armchair by the table in the window. I couldn't help it, she shouldn't have smiled at me like that, as if she was surprised, but pleased to see me. I picked up the lamp and smashed it over her head. She fell on the floor but she didn't really try to stop me, she just reached out a hand. I hit her again and she became unconscious but I didn't want anyone to know what I'd done so I kept hitting her until I was sure she was dead.'

'Then you put the lamp in the bin and went home?'

Susan nodded. 'It was nearly seven o'clock by then so I waited outside the paper shop until it was open. In case anyone had missed me.' Ian found it difficult to imagine how anyone in that position could act so logically, planning an alibi in such a calculated fashion, but he refrained from commenting on it. No one was awake on her return and she continued with the normal routine, breakfast on the table at eight, half an hour later because it was Sunday. But she was worried. She knew Mrs Bedlow had seen her at six fifteen, and that was too early to be going to the paper shop. Even then she was aware it was only a matter of time.

'We know you bought nail polish remover. Was that to remove the evidence?'

Susan nodded. 'I only noticed it later, it was on my skirt, the flowered one. I didn't think it would show but the more I looked at it the more it seemed to stand out.'

'What about the blood?'

'Blood? There wasn't any. Not on me anyway. She fell forward on to the floor and when I hit her again I stood back.' Susan appeared surprised. Did they think she would have sullied herself with that woman's blood?

They went through it all again and again. Susan began to shake, it was a long time since her last Valium tablet. Ian took a deep breath. He was satisfied. There was only one more question to ask and then he would be certain.

'How many times did you hit the deceased, Mrs Barfoot?'

'Eight or nine I think.'

'Thank you. That's all for now. You'll be escorted back to the cells and a doctor'll be along to have a look at you shortly.' Susan Barfoot was led away.

Ian put his head in his hands. 'OK. What now? If she didn't do it, who the hell did?' She had to be protecting someone, and that someone could only be her husband.

MARK WENT OFF TO BED and Moira poured a couple of large whiskies and sat down beside Ian to hear the rest of the story.

'So she confessed to it all this morning. What made you doubt what she said? It all worked out as you thought.'

'Initially, yes. But we knew quite quickly she didn't do it. In her statement she mistook the place where Mrs Henderson had been sitting. John Cotton worked that out from her position on the floor. And there were, believe it or not, only three blows to the head.' Even now it seemed impossible; the physical strength wielded must have been great. 'Maybe someone in a panic could miscalculate by one, or maybe two, but not as many as she did. It was cruel in a way but we withheld her Valium. It still took several more hours of questioning before she broke down.

'We wanted to hear it from her first. I couldn't believe Michael Barfoot was the sort of man to let his wife go to prison for a crime he committed, nor that he was the sort of man to commit it. But we did discover he, too, had problems at university. He suffered, if that's the right word, from very strong sexual urges which he found hard to control. He often fantasized he was raping one of the students. Because he's basically a shy man he didn't discuss this with anyone so never realized such thoughts were not uncommon, but mainly people do not go around living out their fantasies. To sublimate these feelings he turned to the church—he was already a Christian anyway—hoping he could atone for what he thought of as his wickedness. He had these same thoughts about Julia. Susan guessed, of course, and that's why she went to Julia's house so early that Sunday morning.'

'And that's when she saw him, and tried to protect him? I can understand that, if she felt what she'd been doing was so wrong, it was a way of punishing herself.'

Ian took a sip of his whisky. 'No,' he said, 'that's when she saw her son.'

ON FRIDAY MORNING, as Julia's body was being lowered into the ground, Matthew Barfoot was being questioned. Very kindly, very gently. Ian had never seen anyone so terrified in his life. It had taken a long time for Susan to break down but in the end she realized it might be the only right thing to do now. A lot of what she claimed in her statement was true, up to and including getting up on Sunday morning. She heard a noise downstairs, turned over to shake her husband, but he wasn't there. She went downstairs in time to see him leave the house and here her morbid jealousy took over. She thought he was going to see Julia. She did not know that Michael had tossed and turned all night, tormented that *she* might be unfaithful. He wanted to collect his thoughts and went in the opposite direction from Julia's, towards the river where he would not be disturbed. By the time Susan threw on some clothes he was out of sight. She was not concerned about the boys, it was unlikely an intruder would choose that time of day to break in. She wanted to catch them together, to give them a piece of her mind and ask Julia to move away. Or so she said. Ian wondered, knowing how neurotic she was, just what she would have done. When she arrived at Churchill Way she went round to the back. There she lost her nerve. Julia might be innocently sleeping, she would make a fool of herself. She waited, deciding what to do, when she heard the back door open. She lost her nerve completely and hid behind the shed. It was then she saw Matthew leaving and was totally confused. When he was out of sight she went in and found Julia. Wishing her dead was a different matter from finding her so, and worse, knowing her son had killed her. Susan reached down to take Julia's pulse and it was as she picked up her wrist that she smudged the nail varnish. There was no pulse and even Susan knew Julia could not have survived the attack. To protect her son, to try to save her precious respectability, she acted as though nothing was wrong. With remarkable cool she placed the lamp and its shade in the dustbin, hoping the body would not be discovered until after it was emptied the following morning, then stopped at the newsagents on the way home to buy a paper. This was to be her excuse if her husband or son were home before her. Michael was, in fact, still out, but Matthew was home. She heard him in the bathroom, a constant stream of water running from the tap. She knew what he was doing.

Nothing was said. Not then, not later. She tried to pretend it had not happened, but she couldn't. She became more and more tense. It was not her tension which affected Matthew and caused him to be ill, it was his own guilt. But in the end she knew she could not let her son take the blame. She had a very good idea why he did it and knew it was mostly her fault.

When Julia came to Rickenham, Matthew was seven. Sometimes she would take him out, also his brother when he was old enough. From there their relationship grew. It was to Julia he turned with his problems, Julia who listened when things got too much for him at home and he spent more of his time

with her than his mother guessed. Julia was not trying to take him away from her as she believed, she was
simply there as a friend, someone who was doing what
was Susan's responsibility. However, Julia did not
foresee the consequences. She, too, was lonely in her
own way, and it was Matthew she confided in, which
led, one Saturday afternoon when she was feeling
particularly low, to her pouring them both some wine.
They finished the bottle and she realized it was a stupid mistake. She couldn't send the boy home in that
state. Because of his mature ways she often forgot he
was only fifteen. She suggested he sleep for an hour or
so, she'd wake him so he wouldn't be late home. Matthew agreed, not being used to the muzzy feeling. Julia made her second mistake. She lay on the bed beside
him. Matthew couldn't say exactly how it happened or
who made the next move, but he did not think the idea
was in either of their minds when he first went to the
house.

'I'd never done it before,' he sobbed, 'and she was
so beautiful, I couldn't believe it was happening to me.
But it never happened again. I wanted it to but she
wouldn't. She said it was a lovely experience, something we should both remember with fondness, but I
should find someone my own age. She's just like all
the rest. Just like my mother. I thought she was good
and kind, but underneath they're all the same. Mum's
always too busy for me, what with the cleaning,
cleaning, cleaning and the men. She's stupid. She
thinks I don't know. How could she do that to Dad?
And then Julia. After that she didn't want to know.
She said she would tell me things so's I'd understand.
Understand? It made it worse. She said she had af-

fairs, that a woman needed a man that way sometimes. And she could have had me. I'd've looked after her.'

'Matthew,' Ian interrupted. The boy was in full flow. His feelings of distrust and rejection pouring out. But Ian needed to be sure he really had killed her. 'Tell me exactly how it happened.'

'I couldn't sleep for thinking about her. I knew she was going to the wedding and she'd be late home. She told me lots of times if she was out late she got sort of high and couldn't sleep and stayed up working on her articles. Everyone was asleep, I just wanted to talk to her. Honestly. That's all I wanted to do.' Ian had to wait. Matthew slumped forward on to the table, head in his arms. He couldn't bear what was happening to him. When he seemed calmer Ian said 'What happened next?'

'I went in the back door—it was usually open if she was awake—and she was sitting there, doing her nails. I started to beg her to let me come and see her that afternoon, or any time. She got cross and said I was to go home immediately, that Mum and Dad would be worried sick. She spoke to me like I was a kid, as if we'd never done anything. The lamp was there, right behind her, the one her husband gave her. I hit her with it. Three times. Then I left.'

'What happened to the lamp, Matthew?' He looked surprised.

'I don't know. I just dropped it on the floor.'

'All right, son. You won't be allowed to go home you know, but we'll arrange for your parents to come and see you.' Matthew nodded. He no longer cared what happened to him.

'Josh?' he asked. 'Is he all right?'

'I'm sure he is. We'll give the hospital a ring later and let you know. Or your Mum can tell you when she gets back.' Susan had gone there immediately upon her release. He was operated on for appendicitis on Thursday and would have to remain in hospital a few more days.

Matthew was led away.

'What a mess,' Ian said once the tape was switched off. 'The whole family's got problems. That boy didn't stand a chance. Well, it's up to the juvenile courts now but I suspect they'll be lenient when they've heard the whole story. The cool of that woman though, destroying the lamp, buying a paper, I can't believe it.'

'A mother's instinct to protect her young is very powerful you know,' Barry Swan said, surprising everyone in the room with this piece of insight.

'She made the call to take the attention away from her son, the one concerning Clayton. Makes me shudder.' The second anonymous call was nothing more than pure spite. It was made by the mother of the girl who claimed Gerry had sex with her. She read the story in the papers, knew it was the town to which he'd moved and tried to cause trouble. She had no idea he could have known Julia. 'Anyway,' Ian said, 'it's all wrapped up.'

He left the office. Tomorrow would be soon enough to do the paperwork. He had had enough.

As he drove home he thought of all the people Julia's murder had touched, how many lives were altered by it, and felt deep despair when he considered the future of the Barfoot family. Those lives had touched his, too, albeit only for a short time. He must now put them out of his mind. There were other cases, more misery lurking in the future. It was his role to prevent it if possible. Then he remembered Mark.

Matthew was Mark's friend. How would he take the news? There was no easy way to tell him and in the end he would have to sort out his feelings in his own way, but this time it would be Ian who broke the news and Ian who would be there to console him. This time he would not let the boy down.

'I'M HOME,' Ian called as he slung his car keys on the hall table. Moira came out of the kitchen where she was ironing. 'It's only two o'clock. Have you done the paperwork already?' She was aware of Matthew's situation but it was not yet public knowledge and they decided to keep the information from Mark until after he came home from school so they could tell him together before he heard it from another source or the television that evening.

'No, Barry's starting on it. I've had my lot the past week. How long before Mark gets home?'

'A couple of hours. I asked him to come straight back tonight.'

'Well, shall I spend those couple of hours with you?' He smiled. 'Or would you rather I went back to work?'

'Oh, Ian. Come here.'

Then, to the delighted surprise of Detective Chief Inspector Roper, his wife grabbed him firmly by the neck, pulled his head down to hers and kissed him soundly. Then she took him by the hand and led him upstairs to do the very thing Susan Barfoot said she hated so much.

Trade-Off
Maxine
O'Callaghan

First Time In Paperback

A Delilah West Mystery

GIVE HER A SIMPLE MISSING PERSONS CASE ANYTIME

Savvy California P.I. Delilah West hits the horsey set in
Laguna Hills when Benjamin Wylie hires her to find his
missing teenage daughter, Tamra.

Things turn nasty when Delilah discovers the bludgeoned body
of Kate Sannerman, the Wylies' neighbor. Had Tamra witnessed
the murder? Was she another victim? Had she planned to run
off with Kate's husband, now the police's prime suspect?

As the case heats up Delilah's days, a new man puts sizzle into
her nights, and things are getting too hot to handle. But she is
determined to keep her cool, even when trying to thwart a killer
trying to put her on ice—permanently.

"A canny piece of work."   —*The Washington Post*

Available in February at your favorite retail stores.

First Time in Paperback

The Lost Keats
Terence Faherty

An Owen Keane Mystery

FROM KEATS TO A KILLER...

A man with more questions than answers, Owen Keane has one foot in the priesthood, the other in detective novels—a trait that finds him questioning his own vocation. So when a fellow seminarian disappears, Owen sees it as a chance to unravel a mystery, and perhaps his own inner struggles.

But it's not until he meets a descendant of the English poet John Keats that scattered clues fall into place. At the center is a missing sonnet, but from there things turn modern—with marijuana and murder adding to the mystery that becomes deadly as Owen gets closer to the truth...and to a killer with a message just for him.

"A near-faultless performance." —*Publishers Weekly*

Available in February at your favorite retail stores.

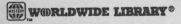